LETHAL LADY

THE LT. VALCOUR SERIES

Murder by the Clock
Somewhere in This House
Murder by Latitude
Murder in the Willet Family
Murder on the Yacht
Valcour Meets Murder
The Lesser Antilles Case
Profile of a Murder
The Case of the Constant God
Crime of Violence
Murder Masks Miami

OTHER MYSTERIES

The Case of the Dowager's Etchings
The Case of the Redoubled Cross
The Deadly Dove
Design in Evil
Diagnosis Murder
Duenna to a Murder
The Faces of Danger
The Lethal Lady
Murder De Luxe
Museum Piece No 13
Murder de Luxe
The Steps to Murder
A Variety of Weapons
A Woman is Dead

SCIENCE FICTION

The Fatal Kiss Mystery

DOG STORIES

North Star: A Dog Story of the Northwest
Whelp of the Winds: A Dog Story

LETHAL LADY

RUFUS KING

WILDSIDE PRESS

Published by Wildside Press LLC.
www.wildsidepress.com

CHAPTER 1

Clara, almost the minute the shock of it got her, turned and followed the woman down to the corner of Rochester Street. That was the way things were about Clara: instantly she would come to decisions whenever chance, and she was a great believer in chance, would throw a sensible answer to a problem into her lap.

This present problem of doing something about her husband, Harold, had been with her for almost a year now. It had been with her like a malignant sort of a fever, fluctuating, intensifying, hidden beneath the mask of her face and behind her clear, truthful-looking eyes. What's more, it had seemed pretty unsolvable until this woman had come along the street and passed her.

You would never believe the sort of woman Clara really was, simply by looking at her. You would just put her down as a very fashionably and expensively turned-out member of the younger matron-and-country-club set, with a solidly handsome estate and a husband who could easily afford both it and her, all of which was perfectly true.

But under it, under this easy and glacé façade, Clara had the amoral appetites of a woman who intends to make a rich pathway for her life no matter what petty irritations, such as flies, have to be killed in order to smooth it. This isn't a bad example, because human beings meant no more to her than flies. As for her age, Clara claimed to be twenty-two.

About her origin nothing was ever disclosed. Certainly she herself never had said anything about it beyond the tritest sort of generalities, and, when the time came really for trying to find out, it was, of course, too late.

At the corner of Rochester Street, the woman paused before Atchinson's drug store and studied an assortment of lotions and cosmetics in its window. Clara paused too, not exactly beside the woman but near enough to observe her profile, and the color of her hair which showed beneath the brim of a bargain-counter hat.

Humid summer sunlight shone down on the pavement with a blistering effect and a hot smell, and from a couple of blocks over in the municipal park, with its lozenge-shaped beds of blatant cannas, a band started blaring one of Sousa's marches as a prelude to the speeches of Farmer's

Day—a political gadget found useful as the first tentative springboard for the fall elections.

The woman had satisfied her curiosity about the display of cosmetics and was aware of Clara, then she grew distinctly aware of Clara, while a certain astonishment filled her eyes.

"It's extraordinary, isn't it?" Clara said. "I had to stop. Do you mind? My speaking, I mean?"

"Yes, I see what you mean."

"Like wearing the same hats."

"Yes, like a mirror."

They were remarkably alike in features and in build, certainly so in age, but their accessories and dress were a good several hundred dollars apart. Clara wondered how swiftly, with what safe degree of abruptness she dared seize this all-but-miraculous stroke of chance, this meeting among the town's fifty thousand inhabitants of a woman who resembled her so closely that she might—yes, it was conceivable that under proper circumstances this woman might pass as her double.

Clara's beautifully controlled smile was warmly intimate while the woman kept on studying her questioningly, at a loss to know what was to happen now, and being a little ill at ease in the face of such obvious *haut couture*—an expression with which she had familiarized herself through the magazine section of her Sunday paper.

The blare of the band over in the municipal park did a final job on Sousa, died into stillness, and the hot, lifeless smell of the streets took over, and the woman said: "Are you going to the speeches?"

"In that crush? I mean even if there weren't a crush. It's bad enough to have my husband using the car while every taxi in town is awash with a politician. Literally, I had to walk. Hairdresser's."

"I feel sort of that way too," the woman said. "About not getting shoved around." She added oddly: "And when there's so many people, there's really nobody."

Clara said impulsively: "This may sound like heat-prostration madness, but won't you have a Collins with me? It will at least remove some of the rancid health from this stilling sunshine, and Blancharde's is just around the corner. My name is Clara Davis."

"Mine is Solda Carmandine. I've nothing else to do, really. So yes, if you like."

They turned the corner, and walked eastward half a block on Rochester Street with its elms, the leaves of which were limp from heat. The trees did not extend beyond a few blocks when the street deteriorated into low cost dwellings (much too low to be, by the city fathers, elmed) and then slid into the heart of the mill section, which sprawled its dull way to the river.

Clara caught a distant sheen of water and absently thought: the river? Then with a growing definitiveness she decided: the river.

Blancharde's was, on the whole, pretty awful, with its bleak façade of glass blocks, like so many eyes of dead fish, while the decor inside, with its completely indirect form of lighting, dissolved any variation between night and day. But it was cool and quiet with that impersonal hush of a tavern during the break in business after lunch, and the speeches had removed all visiting firemen to the grandstand in the park. It had the damp, miasmic smell of countless beers and the faint acridity of dead tobacco.

Clara had only been in the place once before, and then it had been late at night and with a crowd. She felt assured that, so far as the staff was concerned, she would be unknown. She led the way to a banquette and, while pulling off her citron-colored mesh gloves, she studied Solda Carmandine more closely in the crepuscular light.

There were but the faintest variations in features, and the eyes were of a color, and the hair. From the rummage room of her catholic knowledge, Clara dug up the thought that bodies bloat. It was according to the length of time they had been immersed. Floaters, she recalled, was the technical word for it.

Even the off-chance of identifying scars or a birthmark would not matter. Not with Harold. Her nerves knotted as she thought of her husband. They did this every time she thought of Harold specifically, and of how, in her opinion, he had sold her down the river.

"What will it be?" Clara asked. "I'm having a rum Collins—I find them deadlier than gin."

Solda Carmandine smiled slowly back. She was beginning to enjoy Clara and to feel more at ease.

"All right," she said. "I'll have one too."

The waiter, who was a confirmed dyspeptic and a cynic at heart, ambled off. Sisters, he thought. But they didn't act like sisters nor talk like them. With that unique perceptiveness of most waiters he sensed the formal, the recently-met touch. And, of course, the difference in their rigs. It bored him. Okay, okay, long-lost sisters then, like the silent-film days of the Gishes—parted by tragedy, reunited by fate. He wearily gave his order at the bar.

"I've just lost my job," Solda Carmandine said. "A Collins will pick me up."

Well, there it was. In a nutshell, on a platter. This friendly stranger had just lost her job, and the unhappy (for her) fact existed that she looked so mirror-like like Clara.

That is something hard to appreciate: that there actually are women like Clara. The Borgias almost had a copyright on it, and did things in the grand style, but after them you had your mediocre, handy axes and your sash-weights as well as the equally effective if stupid insecticides with a few frills of injected chocolates. Always caught.

Clara had no intention of being caught.

She was a curious woman in the sense that she commingled an exact intelligence with the blindest sort of dependence on Fate. A tea leaf could upset the very clearest of her reasoning powers and she would have been a prime pushover for the Sibyls.

Her superstitions and her trust in portents (claps of thunder, unrising yeast—what have you) were legion, and she collected new ones as avidly as her husband, Harold, collected books. It was curious (Fate?) that, on the very day when some female misanthrope had told her it was unlucky to transplant parsley, Harold should have brought home the early edition of Alfred Lord Tennyson's poems.

Harold had said: Have you ever read him, dear?"

"No."

"Well, there are times when I think that the main requisites for the poet laureatship are stamina and a good second wind."

That had been a month ago, a sulky sort of an afternoon, and Harold had gone out leaving the book lying on a table, and Clara had dipped into it. Tennyson had outraged her as being the deadliest corn, because fundamentally she was an iron-bound realist, but the narrative of Enoch Arden did hold her. She skipped through it at first and then, suddenly, the notion came that there was something in it for her. If, that was, she could handle it right.

She reread the poem carefully from beginning to end. She recalled a few rehashes of its plot which she had seen in the movies: always the vanished husband returned to find his beloved wife married again. This invariably caused him to wallow in a puddle of noblesse oblige and he either died, as per Tennyson, or once more disappeared, this time forever. Lights, handkerchiefs, and tears.

Occasionally (still sticking to Tennyson) there was a child by the bigamous marriage, but one rule had been adamant in every version: it was always the husband who had evaporated. The poor fellow never did this vanishing act consciously, but rather as the result of some cruel mischance—a shipwreck, as Tennyson started the racket, then ranging upwards into the svelter regions of amnesia.

Suppose—the seed had taken root on that past sulky afternoon in Clara's brain, because that was the way in which Clara's brain worked—suppose it were the beloved wife who were, to vanish?

Suppose she, Clara, were to vanish and Harold were to marry again?

In this regard Edna Washburton instantly flashed into her mind: the lifelong friendship of Edna and Harold, Edna's widowhood, Edna's essential *wife*liness—the entire setup in its nice perfection. And then, in proper time, the pay-off, with life's pathway rich and smooth.

But there had been something in the poem about ten years.

Clara had reviewed the passage:

> *...O Annie*
> *It is beyond all hope, against all chance,*
> *That he who left you ten long years ago*
> *Should still be living;...*

Yes, the sterling Annie had certainly hung up some sort of a record or other in non-perishable hope. And wasn't there a law about it? An Enoch Arden law or something? Anyhow, Clara had shelved the plan and the book.

Until now.

CHAPTER 2

The waiter made indifferent gestures toward an indifferent fly. He gave a negligently professional glance toward the two women on the banquette. Sippers. Both of them. Probably one repeat on the collinses and then they'd steam out into the long, hot, deadly afternoon.

"What was your job, Miss Carmandine?" Clara asked.

"I was secretary to Mr. Allwhite at the Frankton Mills. Mr. Allwhite was transferred to their new plant in Georgia, and Mr. Walters took his place, and had his own secretary. I could have stayed but I didn't want to go back into the pool." Solda Carmandine added half apologetically: "After having been with one of the executives, you see."

"Yes, I can understand how you felt."

"Also, there are plenty of jobs and I'd like a vacation for a while. I've wanted a good long vacation for the past several years—you know, or I guess you don't really—but just doing anything you want to, without planning for it. Just everything that comes along. When I was a kid I used to close my eyes and spin around and throw a stone, then I'd walk in the direction it fell, hoping that something new and exciting would happen."

"Did it ever?"

"No, but the feeling was there, and I'd always pretend that it did."

(*Ten years—no, not ten years—no need to wait for ten years now.*)

"Do you live with your family, Miss Carmandine?"

"No, my home was out in Minnesota. Papa's farm is just a few miles from Bethel. I've got a small apartment here on Ashcourt Street. A couple of rooms."

"Alone?"

"Yes. It's one thing I used to long for back in Bethel, real honest privacy. This isn't anything fancy, of course—it's a walkup—but you are let alone. I never see anybody but Mrs. Lovestone when she stops by on the last of the month for the rent. Sometimes she stays a few minutes for coffee and cake."

"Have you talked with her about your plans for a vacation?"

"Yes, I have. Mrs. Lovestone is old. She's fifty. But even at that age she knows what I mean. She's sort of on the romantic side herself, and frustrated."

"How long—do you mind if I call you Solda?"

"Of course not."

"And you must call me Clara. How long do you intend to rest, Solda?"

"Honestly I don't know. Until it stops being novel and exciting, I guess. Novel like being here now with you is one of the things I mean. Just out of a blue sky."

"A very hot blue sky."

"Anyhow it's a mood, sort of like drifting. I guess, at least, it will be for as long as the money holds out."

"Savings?"

"That's right."

Clara said with a perfected shade of indifference: "I suppose you bank at the Merchants National. I know my husband does."

"Lord no, the savings aren't as important as that. Anyhow, I don't like banks. I like to feel that the money's always where I can get at it. Like at home on the farm there was always the cracked teapot."

Solda Carmandine finished the Collins and felt wonderfully peaceful. It was as if she had known Clara for years. The Italians called it sympatico: that elusive but warm suddenness with which in an instant (or after a stiff rum Collins on a scorching day) you had known a person all your life. It was so very comfortable and friendly, like a log fire.

The waiter mused toward them and Clara said: "Again."

"There wasn't any answer to Minnesota," Solda Carmandine said.

"No, I shouldn't think there would be. Mostly dancing on platforms, isn't it?"

"At times, in summer. How do you know?"

"Oh the Swedes, and over-spiced meats."

"But lots of it is just like that!"

"Yes, I've met Swedes."

"I'm not. I'm Italian."

"Yes, the name."

"Half."

"And half Swedish?"

"Well, almost. Mama's folks were pretty nearly everything. She used to make a joke about it and call herself Mrs. Atlas. She's dead, Mama is. She died before I left Bethel. It's the main reason really why I did."

"I suppose you keep in touch with your father and the rest of the family, Solda?"

"Well, no. Not in the way I imagine you mean. I'm an only child and the others are just cousins. Mama almost died when I was born—you know. Anyhow it's about come down to an exchange of Christmas cards.

Papa doesn't even bother with that, but I always send him one just the same."

"Isn't there—haven't you ever felt that you wanted to go back, even for a visit?"

"Well, yes and no. Oh there are times when I've wanted to, ever so much, if it were just to the farm, to the fields, to the smell of them. I can't."

"Really?"

"Papa—well, Papa and I didn't part as friends."

Clara glanced at her watch.

"Let's make this our last drink. It's barely four o'clock and I've an idea. Are you certain that you're not tied up, Solda? You've no one to meet, or anything like that?"

"Not a thing to do in the world."

"I've a camp a few miles out along the river. We'll kill this blazing day with a good, cool swim."

"Oh I'd love to, but I don't know how to swim." Clara's fingers tightened imperceptibly about her glass. She finished the Collins, then she stood up and pulled on her gloves.

"It's easy to learn to swim, Solda. I could teach you how."

CHAPTER 3

Sergeant Walter Morris of the Missing Persons Bureau said: "Mr. Davis, sit down."

"Thank you, Sergeant Morris."

Harold Davis sat in a surprisingly comfortable chair by the desk. It was surprising, because his total lack of knowledge about police affairs in general had led him to visualize a hard-seated, and hard-headed austerity.

Harold was an oddly innocent man for his age, which was forty, about many things such as politics, or machinery, or almost any utilitarian subject—certainly of any of the brutal or earthy facts of life like poverty, or crime, or deadening despair. His father had died when Harold was a child and his mother had brought him up in the most sheltered possible fashion. Her hold had been released two years ago by death, and shortly afterward Clara had decided to marry him.

Clara did.

It had been the most exciting thing that ever had happened to Harold. He had scarcely dared believe in his good fortune that he, already plumping into middle-age, should have netted this lovely and tender young butterfly, for so he had considered Clara.

And then after a while, well possibly the money, the very substantial Davis estate, had started it: Clara's artless dumping it about by bucketfuls. From his first ten-cent piece (half of which had been salted away in a piggy bank) his mother had drilled into Harold the sacred responsibility of wealth. Had he been too stern about this with Clara?

Sergeant Morris was saying: "I believe this is about your wife, Mr. Davis?"

Harold came back to the reality of the comfortable chair and to the pleasant, quietly-spoken younger man across the desk.

"Yes. I haven't seen her since Thursday, nor heard from her. Nobody has. I realize this is Saturday but I kept hesitating—I kept hoping, and ringing up our friends—hoping, perhaps, that there would be some word."

This, initially, struck Morris as thin, but he took a longer look at Harold and then thought it mightn't be, at that. His experience in the bureau had taught him that men frequently lagged in reporting a missing woman, whereas with women the reverse was true. Even a late-for-dinner husband sometimes brought out the troops.

No, there was nothing unique in Harold's type as Morris knew it: carefully bred, probably a procrastinator in making most decisions for himself, the sort of man who would shy violently at personal publicity.

"Had you any reason to feel that your wife might have left you, Mr. Davis?"

"Purposely?"

"Yes. I've found it best to be blunt about these things—with another man?"

Oddly, this had never occurred to Harold. He thought about it now.

"No," he said, "I think I'd have known. You sense that sort of thing intuitively, don't you?"

"I'm afraid not."

"But look here, we were almost constantly together. I mean by that we were together in our mutual social interests and friends. I do admit that just at the start, right after I'd realized she'd gone—there's that difference in our ages, you see. It's almost twenty years."

"Let me put it for you, Mr. Davis. Were you afraid she might just have got tired of you?"

"Frankly, yes. But last night the clothes and her things—I suppose I should have noticed it before."

"She had left everything?"

"The fact suddenly struck me that she had—her bags—her toilet articles—those things. I mean it was driven home to me that she hadn't *planned* to go away."

Again Morris felt a thinness, and again he took a careful look at Harold. Dreamer? The professor type? Congenitally absent-minded? A nice fellow, and the sort Morris felt it would be pleasant to know off and on. "How about her jewelry?" he asked.

"Oh yes, she left those too—several good pieces of her own and quite a few that I had given her."

"What about money?"

"My wife has no bank account of her own that I know of. She's young and has the reckless disregard of values which you find in youth."

"I'm trying to get at about how much actual cash she might have had in her bag."

"It couldn't have been much. She has charge accounts for anything she might want to buy. Within reason, that is."

"Just how old is your wife, Mr. Davis?"

"Clara is twenty-two. Here's a picture of her. I thought you might want one."

Morris looked at the cabinet photograph, then put it down on the desk. There was something off the beam all right. She wasn't the type who would go dewy-eyed and wholesome over a Davis, with that age span of twenty years.

"How about her measurements?"

Harold looked slightly shocked.

"I wouldn't—I'm quite sure I don't know."

"Has she any birthmarks or scars?"

The flush on Harold's cheeks deepened.

"About that too I couldn't say."

"Well, her parents probably know."

"No, Clara told me that they were dead. Our both being alone—I think it was one of the things that first drew us together. My mother, you see, had but recently died."

"Where was your wife born, Mr. Davis?"

"I don't know. I met her in New York while settling up some angles of my mother's estate. I suppose it may be difficult for you to understand this, Sergeant Morris, but I've never asked her anything about her family or her background."

"No, there's no difficulty in understanding. Such things are entirely a matter of situation and temperament. Did you meet her through mutual friends?"

"As a matter of fact we met by the oddest chance. Clara always says that Fate was responsible for it. There's a restaurant I like when I'm in New York, a little French place on east Fifty-fourth Street. Snails. She was eating alone there, and after a while she smiled. Well—"

"Where did she live in New York, Mr. Davis?"

"At that girls' club in the west fifties—the Arts or something."

"Yes, I know."

Morris felt that the picture was reasonably clear, just a run-of-the-mill setup: Davis held tight to the purse strings, Davis was set in his ways, and his young wife had just got fed up with him and his middle-aged crowd.

"What was her business in New York?"

"She was studying for the theater."

"Had she been in any shows?"

"No, just studying."

"She must have had some source of private income then."

"There again—I mean I suppose you are right, but I—we never discussed it. Girls do come to the city looking for a career—they have a nest egg of sorts and plunge it—hoping—"

Morris, because he continued to like him and had decided he was sound, began to feel uncomfortable for Harold too. He said: "Tell me about the last time you saw her on Thursday."

"Well, we had breakfast—my house is just outside of town on the country club road—it's that sort of a large brick one of heaven knows what period."

"I know the one you mean. I've noticed it when I've passed it. Fine trees around it."

"They are, aren't they? So many people object to locusts—think they're dirty, because they shed those delightful petals in the spring. They've an odor, you know. Very delicate, but awfully fine."

This was all very well, but there was too much of it. "You were having breakfast, Mr. Davis?"

"Oh yes, and I asked Clara whether she minded my using Patterson and the town car until quite late that night. My own car was being repaired—parts of the engine or something had started dropping out—and I wanted to see Tommy Whitfield over in Luthertown about a first edition of Stephen Crane."

"Just what is your business, Mr. Davis?"

"I haven't any."

"I take it that after breakfast you left, and that was the last you saw of her?"

"Yes."

"When you came back"—Morris glanced at his notes—"late that night, and found her gone, what did you do?"

"But I didn't know then. It was after one o'clock and the door to her room was closed. I just went to bed and then, when she didn't come down in the morning for breakfast, and her bed hadn't been slept in, well, that's when I knew she was gone."

"What had the servants to say about it?"

"We've only two, outside of Patterson, that is. A cook and a maid. They're both awfully old. They were with Mother for almost as long as I can remember. Clara—I mean we both have tried to keep a reasonable staff but, well it just seems as though they won't stay."

"What did the cook and the maid have to say, Mr. Davis?"

"Just that Clara had had lunch at home and then had started out to walk to town for an appointment at her hairdresser's. She tried to telephone for a taxi but I suppose, because it was Farmers Day, she couldn't get one."

"Did they say what she was wearing?"

"No, I didn't ask them."

"Do, please, when you get home, and telephone me and let me know."

"I will."

"What else did they say?"

"Why nothing, really. As I've said, they're both very old, and I'm sure they sleep most of the afternoon. When Clara wasn't home for dinner they just took it for granted she was dining with friends, so they went to bed."

"How about her friends in New York?"

"I never met any."

"Surely there must have been some correspondence?"

"No, I can't remember Clara ever having got a letter from New York."

"Well, from anywhere? Surely, Mr. Davis, everyone has certain ties, links with their past?"

"Sergeant Morris, I know this must seem absurd, but again it's the way I feel about things. Naturally, for a while I thought it strange that Clara got no letters, and then I thought she simply wanted to cut out the earlier part of her life completely."

"Will you stand up, please, Mr. Davis?"

Harold, somewhat bewildered, stood up from the comfortable chair. "Just stand?"

"Yes, please." Morris also stood up. "Show me about where the top of your wife's head came to. You, I should judge, are about five feet eleven?"

"Just, and Clara came to about here, just about to my chin."

"Thank you. That will give us a reasonable approximation of her height. Is this photograph a recent one?"

"It was taken last January."

"All right, Mr. Davis. We'll do the best we can, and we'll let you know."

Harold hesitated about leaving.

"Would you—could you form any notion, Sergeant Morris?"

"Several, and naturally none of them is pleasant. You can understand that."

"Yes?"

"An accident resulting in hospitalization or something worse can be checked. There is always the possibility of amnesia, either temporary or permanent. It seems that amnesia is getting increasingly popular these days—sort of a who-am-I? wave. Are you a rich man, Mr. Davis?"

"Well yes, I suppose I am."

"Then we cannot disregard kidnapping."

"But isn't there always a ransom note?"

"The techniques vary. You will hear from us as soon as anything turns up."

"And if nothing should turn up, like those cases, like the Crater case?"

Sergeant Morris held out his hand.

"Telephone me that description of her clothes, Mr. Davis, and I suggest that you hope for the best."

CHAPTER 4

Mrs. Lovestone, in whose roomy old-fashioned building Solda Carmandine kept her two-room apartment, hesitated before Solda's door. The narrow hallway was completely quiet, and the rooms behind the closed door were very quiet too. They had been so since Thursday, with none of the slight occasional sounds which assured you that someone was inside.

They were the trivial sounds of living which Mrs. Lovestone had been accustomed to hear on her passage along the hallway to the floor above where she had her own quarters, and through the floor of which she had been able to hear a faint infiltration of Solda's radio during the early evenings. She scarcely could recall a nine o'clock without having heard Solda dial in the *Tale of Lost Loves* hour on WLQD.

She was familiar with Solda's dreamed-of plans for a good long vacation of the most flotsam and carefree sort, but if the vacation were actually now in effect it struck Mrs. Lovestone as queer that Solda hadn't said goodbye.

This lifelessness, an emptiness, impelled Mrs. Lovestone toward the resolution that something ought to be done, even to the extent of an intrusion on that privacy which she knew her tenant insisted upon so passionately.

Mrs. Lovestone rapped on the door and then, after a polite while, rapped again. She called softly: "Miss Carmandine?" Their relationship had always remained on a socially formal stratum. She used her passkey and went inside.

The rooms were neat, which Mrs. Lovestone had expected. They were also empty. This brought her an initial sense of relief. A dead Solda had not seriously occurred to her, but the thought had hesitated in the back of her mind. So many solitary people did have things happen to them, and usually it would be days before the things were found out.

Solda's bags were not in the cupboard, nor were her clothes, nor were any of her articles of personal use, either on the dresser or in the medicine chest of the small bathroom. It dawned on Mrs. Lovestone that there was nothing of Solda around at all. The desk also had been emptied, with the exception of a plain white envelope on its let-down front.

Mrs. Lovestone opened the envelope. Solda's key to the apartment and forty dollars were inside it. The money covered the past month's rent and would have been due on the day after tomorrow, Monday. Mrs. Lovestone was becoming a little angry and hurt.

She thought back to Thursday. Yes, it had been that night, very late that night, say toward three o'clock in the morning when she had waked with the sleepy impression of a car outside on the street, of a curious minor noise on the stairway as if, say, a suitcase had bumped against a banister. The sound had been much too evasive to warrant getting out of bed, of fully waking oneself up and then having to bother about getting to sleep again.

Mrs. Lovestone was now somewhat madder and deeply offended. She locked the apartment and went on up to her own quarters where she telephoned the *Blush Falls Gazette*. She asked for the advertising department and then said to Bella, who ran it and whom she knew very well: "Bella, one two-room-and-bath for rent, same price as usual—yes, dear, for immediate occupancy. Who? Oh, Solda Carmandine had it. You wouldn't know her. I guess nobody does, really. She was the lonely type."

Having attended to this, the anger and resentment, the hurt feeling at Solda's brusque departure began to abate. It was so out of character, the ladylike character Mrs. Lovestone had found her tenants to be during the coffee-and-cake sessions when both had come to know each other with a certain (elevated) degree of intimacy.

Bethel, Wisconsin—no, Minnesota—that was where Solda had been born and where her father now lived, an R.F.D. outside-of-town address. Write?

Could it have been romance?

Mrs. Lovestone who had never experienced the slightest bit of it was, as Conrad initiated the cliché, incurably romantic. Her husband, now dead, had been an occasional salesman of occasional objects. He had had a moustache and hair on his fingers, a noisy way of eating, without even an extended little finger, and the whole thing had certainly not been romance.

Maybe Solda, with her solitude and obscure ways, had found it and had, on that now aging Thursday night, eloped—without having had anyone to elope from except Mrs. Lovestone to whom she should have said goodbye. Yes, it could well be that. Mrs. Lovestone decided not to write.

Just let the matter rest.

CHAPTER 5

Edna Washburton, with placid dignity, snipped the dead heads from her roses. She used the special scissors which held them, with a measure of tender regret, and then dropped them into the Aztec basket. Her garden, with its pools of sunshine and banks of shade, was completely proper and charming, just as Edna was proper and charming.

She had no distinctive beauty, but her features, and carriage, and absolute taste in dress all summed up into giving Edna what has always been accepted as the patrician look. Forty years had left untouched her tall, slim figure, with an effect of willowiness in all of her movements. Some carpers called this planned but it wasn't true, for Edna was a thoroughly natural woman.

Her life had been a very placid one. Even her husband's death, five years ago, had been accompanied by no strongly emotional upsets, no devastating grief, because there had been so little of the flame, the warm true flame which causes it.

Edna, after the high Episcopalian funeral and imperceptible descension of the coffin into the grave, had just quietly continued on in her well-run, very Victorian house (the grounds of which adjoined the Harold Davis estate) peacefully indulging her two hobbies, which were gardening, and her simple attacks on Chopin—who certainly didn't mind any longer what she did to his Etudes.

However there were occasional moments when Edna would feel, just as Mrs. Lovestone had felt, that she had missed something in life. Frankfort Hamilton Washburton had been coldly, correctly serene. A banker, and a very nice person, but as exciting as a perfectly-done omelet, which once one had eaten it, everything was solid and substantial but where were you? Nourished. And at such compatibly Lovestone moments Edna would invariably think, in a nice indeterminate fashion, about Harold Davis.

They had grown up together, she and Harold, on their families' neighboring estates. That is to say they had grown up as much together as Harold's mother had permitted. Lawn tennis, croquet, dancing school (the gavotte was still in)—all of the simple amusements which required daylight or the inclusion of other children of their age. But there had been no hayrides under any hunter's moon, nor any driftings in a canoe along the moonlit river to the accompaniment of a ukulele and the soft sweet melodies of that bygone day.

Often since her husband had died Edna wondered just what it was she still felt about Harold. Her innate propriety and thoroughly conventional nature prevented her from wondering *too* deeply because of Harold's (startlingly) having become a married man and going almost so determinedly overboard about the so-much-younger Clara.

It had been something of a shock to Edna, this marriage of spring and almost-fall, as it had been to all of Harold's friends, but Edna had understood it better than the others because she understood more clearly what Harold's maternally enveloped life had been: that constant assurance that mother-knows-best. Edna had just chalked the marriage off as a rebound in the extreme.

She stopped her dead-head snipping, as she saw Harold walking towards her along a garden path. He looked awfully done in and, well, indeterminate.

"I've just come from the Missing Persons Bureau," Harold said. "It's odd how very nice they are. Edna, could I have a highball? I'm very tired. I'm tired of this continuing bewilderment. Where on earth, and why, is she?"

Well, there wasn't anything that Edna could say about that. She simply couldn't, as the bulk of his friends cared to do, congratulate him on the happenstance that Clara was gone, no matter how or where or why, but at any rate gone out of his life like an interluding fever.

"Roses have always astonished me," she said, clutching at something to say. "I mean they have the appearance of such complete fragility but at heart, Harold, they're awfully tough. These, the ones over here, will still bloom when snow is on the ground. It's just something about them."

Edna herself didn't know just what she was talking about (certainly Harold didn't) but she felt this about roses—they were right things with lovely fragrance which could still stand up against the rigors of a deadly frost—not like Clara—

A maid brought them drinks on the terrace, and Harold stretched out gratefully on a wicker chaise shaded by a cork tree with its angular lines and flat-held leaves. How comfortable it was here, what orderliness, and what peace! He felt it treacherous that this should be so, what with Clara having gone heaven-knew-where, or under what tragic caprice of circumstances.

But it was there, this—yes, almost this sense of release: a release from the exacting strain which living with Clara had mountingly brought him under, and which he had been terrified she might ever discover. It was the strain of a constant attention to his appearance, in order to negate the gap between middle-age and youth, the early risings (on his part) to shave, to comb his thinning, tousled hair, to modify the gracelessness of the inexorable years, in fact all of his trivial but studied graspings after being again companionably young.

Harold thought of these things now, in the pleasant shade, in the contemporary and so-long-familiar charm of Edna—how long ago, what ageless years it seemed since bob-sledding and pulling her pig-tailed head out of the snow, the birthdays with angel cake and the gone-forever number of little candles. Would there ever be such cakes again, even if there were room enough for the candles in their icing-rosebud holders— and he thought: This is horrible, this is despicable, to think right now of things such as these.

"Sergeant Morris—he's of the Missing Persons Bureau, Edna—he said just to mark time and that he'd let me know."

CHAPTER 6

On the Thursday following the one of Clara's disappearance, the usual small boys who were fishing along the riverbank came upon the usual discovery, and ran howling to their mothers. The gist of their shrieks amounted to the fact that a lady without a stitch on her, and considerably swollen, was floating face down among the rushes, with her hair like little snakes in the backwash of the current.

The law moved, both city and county, and in a reasonably short time it involved Sergeant Morris into covering a possible identification from the missing persons' files. The lady was under a sheet on an ambulance stretcher by the time Morris reached the spot.

Morris looked. He studied the hair, the now hideous eyes, the swollen features and the general overall of size. He looked for rings: a wedding ring, an engagement ring. There was none.

He said to the medical examiner: "Does it look like a plain drowning?"

"There's nothing else so far. I'll do a *p.m.* tonight. Could she be on your list?"

"I think she is. She could be a Clara Davis. How long would you say she'd been in, at a guess?"

"At a guess, for about a week."

"That would check too. Davis reported his wife was missing since last Thursday."

Morris moved over to the bank and studied the outer current, then the nearer eddies and this rush-laden backwash of the river. From one of the camps, of course. At night. You didn't go Godiva with the sun up.

He chatted for a while with various members of the department, of the sheriff's office, the county prosecutor's and the state police. Then he got into his car, and slowly drove in a direction opposite the river's flow along the river road towards town. In most places you rode close to the bank, and only lost sight of it when occasional spits of land jutted out into the water.

Mostly there were camps built on these spits and, as he passed them, Morris read the names of their owners, either on R.F.D. mail boxes or on variously designed signs, most of which were abominably cute. Harold Davis's camp was the seventh on the way into town.

Morris stopped the car. It was none of his business, as his sole connection with the case was to assist in establishing an identification of the body, but he was an ambitious man and there were his wife Freda and his two children to consider, and he had no intention whatever of becoming grooved in the identification bureau for the rest of his life. He wanted, when those seemingly endless years of old age would arrive, for Freda and for him to have papayas, a lemon tree, and a boat for beguiling tarpon.

He turned the car into a driveway densely flanked with evergreens and drew up before the verandah of a pleasant and typical log-cabin house, the modern sort which would have sent an early settler into gasps. The lock of the front door yielded easily to a master key.

Morris went into a big room which was conventionally rigged out with a fieldstone fireplace and the rugged sort of expensive furniture that looks comfortable but never quite manages to be so. The air was hot and stale, but the light was good, as the outside shutters had not been closed.

The room appeared reasonably lived in, with magazines at convenient places, one being opened face down on a table beside a lounge chair. It was a woman's magazine and the story an effective and ever-gripping marital problem. 'No,' Morris read, 'you cannot do this to me and I—I cannot do this to *her*!' Her, being taken for granted by Morris as the cold hard wife, like the general impression of landladies who also were always cold and hard, because even they, when you came right down to it, had to live which meant eat.

The hearth was clean. An ash tray contained ashes on the table beside the open magazine, but no cigarette butts. The fact made no sense, unless you thought about it. The cushions, on a lounge near the fireplace, were still indented from having been leaned against, by, Morris thought, two people.

There were two bedrooms, each having twin beds, and each having its cupboard in both of which were hanging an ordinary assortment of camp clothes and swim suits, Harold Davis's in one and Clara Davis's in the other…

There were two swim suits in Clara Davis's cupboard, one white and one canary yellow. Both were of some rubbery material and consisted of abbreviated shorts and equally skimpy halters, with two color-matching bathing caps of rubber.

The twin beds in her room were smoothly made, as had been those in Harold's.

The one bathroom was clean and neat, with face, and bath towels folded over their racks.

A combination kitchen and dining room showed no disorder; nothing was soiled or out of place; the garbage container was empty. An electric refrigerator was running. Its shelves held ten bottles of beer, three quart bottles of sparkling water, and a half-filled bottle of ginger ale with a rubber cork in it. No cubes were missing from the ice trays.

Morris went out and locked the door.

He thought: Could be.

He thought: It's queer.

No rings.

And everything so neat.

CHAPTER 7

On his farm outside of Bethel, Minnesota, Antonio Carmandine gathered the morning's mail from a roadside box. He was a brute of a man in his late fifties, his shock of black hair still unflecked. His shoulders and arms were heavy with power, and his muscular middle very flat.

His capacity for rage was enormous, either for the long-smoldering or the flash pan sort. He rarely exercised the latter as people with whom he came into argumentative contact, after a spatter of broken noses and crushed ribs, generally let him have his way.

Carmandine looked through the mail as he walked back from the highway along a short dirt road which led to a solid and helplessly unimaginative house. Its lines were the essence of utility, and it made you think of an over-washed face on a homely woman.

In the mail were some seed catalogs for fall plantings, a notice from the fanners' co-operative, a bill from the telephone company, and an envelope postmarked Blush Falls. Antonio Carmandine studied the handwriting on this one. It wasn't Solda's but it was, he thought, a woman's.

Solda must be either sick or in some trouble. The possibility of either of which pleased him. He came to the conclusion that, if she were dead, the address would have looked more official, more masculine, and in all probability it would have been typewritten. Carmandine considered his deductive powers remarkably acute, and he never missed the pleasure of indulging in them. The fact that they never hit within a mile of their target he was accustomed to brush aside. He tossed the mail onto a porch rocker and walked back to the henhouses to continue the morning chores with his two hired helpers, both of whom cordially loathed him.

At noon, Carmandine's fat housekeeper served him, and the hired help, and herself one of her uninspiring but most filling meals, heavily based on noodles and meat balls spiced to their last ground. During it the conversational heights which were reached remained at their usual nadir, being packaged into a continuous sluffing and a few grunts.

After the conclusion of a hefty pudding concocted out of three types of stale bread, prunes, citron and suet—the whole horrible thing being steamed and ultimately sauced with a milk vanilla—Carmandine went out onto the porch, picked up his mail, and sat down.

He opened the telephone bill which, because it meant shelling out money, interested him keenly, and then the notice from the co-operative, which also was of interest but much less so. The seed catalogues held his attention only so far as a speculative eye tour of their garish covers, with prospective vegetables, which could only conceivably have sprung from the upper Saks.

The letter postmarked Blush Falls was signed by a woman named Adelia Lovestone. The name meant nothing to him whatsoever, beyond that it must, in some irritating fashion, be concerned with Solda.

Carmandine had had no use for his daughter since the day when she had collected the small inheritance her mother had left her and had, in turn, left home—at the very time, of all times, when a woman's work (5 a.m. to 8 p.m.) was most needed to be done.

Solda had had the further unkindness to defy him and to refuse to turn over to him the money which her mother (his own wife, mind you) had bequeathed, and this atrocious stand had been further taken after Carmandine already, in his mind's eye, had invested it in a new tractor. He still became hot and muscle-bunched whenever he thought about it, and his eyes would recede while cords in his thick neck swelled.

He read:

My Dear Ms. Carmandine,

Your dear daughter Solda may have written to you of me. She has had a sweet little nest in my house for the past year or so and I have come to think of her as a real friend—as much so, that is, as she will permit anyone to have her friendship.

She makes such a *fetich* out of privacy as you, her father, doubtlessly must know!

(Carmandine's ever-active blood pressure steadily mounted, as he wondered why in blazes she didn't get to the point. And what was a *fetich*? It sounded like a foreign dish.)

Your daughter flew away from her little nest several days ago and evidently has meant to give it up as she left me her last month's rent money and took all of her belongings with her—just folding her tents like the Arabians and stealing away into the night. Last Thursday night. It struck me as so odd, both her manner of going and the fact that she didn't even say good-by!

(At this point Carmandine decided that Adelia Lovestone, with her tent-folding Arabians, was a fossilized, demented old fool.)

At first I decided to respect your daughters evident wish for privacy and presumed she was, because of her almost furtive departure, merely indulging in her *fetich*—but a little matter has come up. Her milk bill, for the last week she was here, has not been paid. As I have no means of getting in touch with her I thought she just *might* have run home for a visit with you. How strong, dear Mr. Carmandine, is the pull of the old homestead in all of us!

If Solda is there will you please ask her to forward me one dollar and eighty-five cents? ($1.85)

Or if she isn't, and you happen to know her present address, will you write me it? And if you don't, will you be so kind as to send me the amount due ($1.85) as the milkman is getting anxious about it?

Very truly yours,

ADELIA LOVESTONE

In the pig's eye I will, decided Carmandine.
He tore the letter into shreds.

CHAPTER 8

Sergeant Morris sat down in the chair which Harold indicated. They were near a window in the living room, one which overlooked what had been a formal garden during Harold's mother's lifetime. It seemed ragged now, and frowzily unkempt. Wild flowers, even though they were very charming wild flowers, were giving it a hedgerow effect. Also, weeds. With little charm at all.

Schulter, the gardener, had left about a month after Clara's installation. She had wanted a mass of exotic blooms, ones impossible for the New England climate with its short growing season (you stuck to peonies, delphinium, phlox—only the sturdiest of the perennials) and its early, killing frosts.

Schulter, being as most gardeners a rugged individualist, had not argued. He had simply muttered something profoundly horticultural about moving the garden to Mexico, a still-muttered sideswipe about seed catalogue virus and fanciful women in general, and had packed. His successors hadn't been any good and even they, bad as they were, hadn't stayed. Not with Clara.

"I think I know what you're going to tell me," Harold said.

Morris, looking at Harold and still wanting to know him off and on, said: "Yes, people get a thing like this intuitively."

"Clara is dead."

Harold said it because he was so very sure of it. He had really been sure from the discovery of Clara's—well, you could call it her extraordinary absence. But here, now, was the ghastly thing, like a documented fact.

Morris said, "It isn't sure, of course, but I'm pretty sure. Most things check. You'll have to make the identification."

"Yes."

"I'm sorry about it."

"I think I've felt right from the beginning that it would be like this. Not consciously, but you know the thought was always there in the back of my mind."

"They found her by the bank, downstream from your camp."

"In the river?"

Harold said this stupidly, and with a certain amazement. He remembered the swift or lazy perfection of her in the water, the dives with then rotogravure perfection and eclectic names. He said: "But Clara could swim. She swam very well."

"You've no idea how many first-rate swimmers drown."

"Cramps? Or I suppose hitting something while diving?"

"You couldn't begin to complete the list of reasons. There's always something new." Morris hesitated for a moment before adding: "This was something new."

"New?"

"It was probably the result of panic—what with cramps or something, maybe in her legs. You know that rocky ledge just below your camp? It goes straight up from the water?"

"Yes, I know where you mean."

"They think she must have tried to clamber up and couldn't make it—nails all broken and fingertips badly abraded. Makes it tough in a way because finger-prints are usually taken for a positive identification—could check them with her toilet articles here, stuff like that, but of course it isn't necessary. You'll know. They feel it must have been at night because she was nude, Mr. Davis."

A deep flush covered Harold's white face.

"That was a habit of hers on moonlight nights, on hot summer nights. I never joined her on them. I don't care for swimming, unless the sun is good and warm."

"I'm sort of that way myself. I suppose you did take a look for her out at the camp after you realized she was missing?"

"Oh yes. I telephoned there on Friday morning but there wasn't any answer, so I took a run out."

"How long did you stay there?"

"I didn't stay at all. I just saw that she wasn't in any of the rooms, so I left and hurried back here. I kept feeling all during those first few days that I ought to be right here near the telephone in case she called, or anybody called."

"Perfectly natural, Mr. Davis. Who takes care of the camp?"

"Care?"

"Yes, keeping it in order—oh you know. Do your servants go out and do it?"

"No, when mother was living I'd manage it myself, but Clara's always done it since we were married. Why?"

"I simply wondered. It seemed in such good shape."

"That's one thing about Clara, she does like orderliness." The truth hit grimly that she did. That she was dead. "I mean—"

"I know. It takes time to realize. Do you feel up to going down to the morgue right now? I could drive you there and back."

"Yes—certainly."

Morris drove him to the morgue. Harold looked at the tragic, bloated face. This couldn't be that young, that pretty thing. But it was. He struggled desperately for control and managed, after a nauseating moment, to achieve a measure of it.

He said: "It's Clara."

CHAPTER 9

The *Blush Falls Gazette* had a special edition on the streets by noon. Mrs. Lovestone opened a copy of it after settling herself in the breakfast nook of her kitchen for a nutritious lunch of almost-Waldorf salad, cinnamon buns and iced coffee.

A front-page cut of the cabinet photograph of Clara Davis loomed up at her almost with the impact of a shocking physical blow. Solda Carmandine—but Mrs. Lovestone's eyes took in the fashionable dress, which was so patently beyond the reach of her former tenant's budget, and then the caption relieved her further: Socialite Mrs. Harold Davis Victim of Accidental Drowning.

But how *much* like Solda Carmandine!

She sped through the story, coming to a slow check at: ...*according to the medical examiner, Mrs. Davis is believed to have met her death on the night of Thursday, August 16. Mr. Davis, still bearing up bravely under the shock and strain, admitted his wife's fondness for taking occasional moonlight swims from their luxurious camp on the river road*...

Mrs. Lovestone figured dates. Yes, the sixteenth was the identical Thursday night on which Solda Carmandine had gone away. She recalled the faint bumping noise, like a suitcase striking a banister, which she had heard at three in the morning, the sound of a car being braked outside on the street. It *was* a curious coincidence, and also there existed that unbelievably strong resemblance.

A brown study held her while she finished lunch, washed the dishes and put things away. So many extraordinary things did happen. She was a sitting duck for clichés, and thoroughly believed that truth was so much stranger than fiction. Her library was largely made up of "Trues," except for a few sentimental and fragrant and utterly worthless eighteenth editions of the turn-of-the-century ladies.

But this.

Well, something should be done. She cut the picture of Clara Davis and the article from the paper, and sat down at the desk.

Dear Mr. Carmandine,

You will be surprised to hear from me so shortly after my previous little note but I do think the enclosed news item and picture are so *odd*, don't you?

I mean that the unhappily drowned Mrs. Davis looks so much like your dear daughter.

And when you consider that the drowning occurred on the identical night when Solda simply faded away I can think of only one thing—Kismet!

I simply couldn't *resist* sending them to you so that you could send them to her—to her Shangri-La, to whatever fuller little nest she has flown to.

I will also take this opportunity of refreshing your memory about the unpaid milk bill for one dollar and eighty-five cents ($1.85) in case it should have slipped your mind.

Very truly yours,

ADELIA LOVESTONE

Mrs. Lovestone licked an envelope and then a stamp. Her fingers, which were inclined to be pudgy, pressed. She put on a shapeless straw hat the crown of which was bedizened with a circlet of forget-me-nots and then started downstairs.

Mr. Loftus Suffern, troubleshooter for Amalgamated Knitting, met her on the landing below. He was a conservatively brash and breezy thirty, with an excellent war background, and an unhappy penchant for hand-painted ties.

"I was just coming up to see you, Mrs. Lovestone."

"Oh yes, Mr. Suffern?"

"I've been called back to the New York office and I'm taking the two o'clock train. I appreciate that you took me on a monthly basis, so here's the balance for the next three weeks."

"Well thank you, Mr. Suffern."

"Not at all. Very nice place you've got here. Very well-run. I'm sure you'll have no trouble in renting."

"No, no trouble at all. As a matter of fact, I rented it to you the very day after the previous tenant, a Miss Carmandine, left."

"Well, I'll say good-by, as I may not be seeing you again."

"Good-by, Mr. Suffern."

Mrs. Lovestone continued down the stairs. She went outside into the morning sunshine, while thinking that sunshine, rain, or the sharp lash of sleet meant nothing whatever any more to Mrs. Harold Davis. What a cruel thing. I mean, Mrs. Lovestone thought, it would have been so much kinder if she had had a bathing suit on. Her sense of the proprieties were practically those of Victoria, and the fact that Mrs. Davis had died was almost secondary to the condition in which from a fairly detailed description in the *Blush Falls Gazette* she had been found.

Well, it was the modern age—a gadget on which Mrs. Lovestone hung most of her dead niceties. She mailed the letter. She bowed to Mrs. Bilchers across the street, then headed for the newspaper office to ask Bella to put the usual in, about the apartment being vacant.

She was bemused over the abruptness of the two departures from it, first Solda Carmandine and now that rather breezy and nice Mr. Suffern. Since her childhood days, when an Irish cook had injected her with the major superstitions, she was sure that the unusual always went in threes.

Idly Mrs. Lovestone wondered: who next? Who would be the tenant and what would happen to him or her?

CHAPTER 10

The sun was dipping down into late afternoon when Morris turned into the office of the Imperial Cab Company. He said to the young woman who handled and dispatched all daytime calls: "I'd like to ask you a foolish question, Elsie."

"What about, Walt?"

"Would there be any chance of checking the fares on last Thursday?"

"Farmers Day? I doubt it. I could give you the ones that were phoned in, but there were any number of pickups. You know what a mob there was. The boys are hardly over it even yet."

"I said it was sort of a foolish question."

"Anyone special, Walt?"

"Yes, a Mrs. Harold Davis. You may have seen her picture in the *Gazette*. I've got a clearer one here."

Elsie looked at it.

"I know," she said. "I read it. What's the angle, Walt? Or shouldn't I ask? It was down as an accident."

"Which it possibly was, but you know me, Elsie. Curious. She couldn't get a cab to go to the hairdresser's, but the walk from her house wasn't so far. The walk to the camp on the river road would have been plenty far. Either some friend, or somebody gave her a lift, or she took a cab. I've been just wondering whether she was alone."

"Well, I'll do my best, Walt."

"Thanks, Elsie."

Morris left and went to Edmonde's over on Maple Street. It was the fashionable beauty establishment of the town, handling the better waves, sets, dos, rinses and what-have-you in a salon of almost quilted mauve. Edmonde himself (he had devised the name on waking up one morning after a terrific bat, also he was supposed to be Parisian but in reality had come from a small village in the province of Quebec) was a tough, volatile, middle-aged man with the most sensitive fingers in the world. He never smiled. His customers loved him.

"Sure thing," he said to Morris. "Sure she was here last Thursday. Maybe around half past one. You want me to look it up in the book?"

"No. Who took care of her?"

"Me. She would not be caught dead with anybody else. Personally I would always have left her to one of the gills. She had not the—the, how in blazes can you say it, the manner? Background? That something which makes an artist willing to exert himself for somebody—even an ugly somebody? But she had the Davis cash. I charged her double."

"What did she talk about?"

Edmonde produced one of his Parisian-Province-of-Quebec shrugs.

"Banalities. The heat—dear Harold having been a pig about the car, with his blistering first editions—no taxis—creeping servants—good God what *do* they talk about?"

"What I'm after is whether she seemed about the same as usual."

Edmonde thought this over.

"They think it might have been suicide?"

"They're thinking it was accidental and leaving it to the inquest. When did she leave here?"

"After three. About half-past. She tried to call a taxi but it was that fantastic Farmers Day and nothing doing."

"Did she say where she was going? Any plans?"

"She said she was sick to death of the heat, the day, Blush Falls, and that she might drop in on Fifi Desmond for a drink, if she could flag a scooter to take her there. She tipped me two bucks."

"Well thanks, Edmonde."

"Okay Walt—anytime you want a permanent."

"And anytime you want a good southern exposure in the cooler."

"Okay."

Fifi Desmond's house was one of those dear old things ("Perfectly *priceless*, darling, nowadays—I mean what with labor and the cost of material you couldn't even *think* of building it—I mean the walls are *that thick!*") from which everything, such as front porches, had been shucked and then a few discreet touches gentled on. Its fireplaces drew beautifully and its roof, on the slightest provocation, leaked beautifully too. Somebody or other, during colonial times, had once slept there.

Fifi was a dear middling thing too. Her role in Blush Falls' society was that of the extra woman, because she had an excellent grip on contract bridge, and the abysmally happy habit of usually losing. Furthermore, she lost well, because she was a nice woman.

"Don't sit on that thing," she said to Morris, judging his heft, "or you, and it, will be on the floor."

Morris smiled back at her, and settled for a lounge. "Clara didn't come here last Thursday," she said. "I wish I could help you. I liked Clara. I liked her because she was direct. I always felt there was something—something very *definite* that she wanted of life. Funny-tragic now—I always felt she'd get it. That's bathos, isn't it? I'll be honest and say that I felt she married Harold for a purpose—money, of course—security—all of his friends did. I mean none of us picture Harold as a romantic character. He's too nice. And I'm not disparaging Clara, because I really did like her. She was a person. She made a bargain and kept it."

"You will go to the funeral, Miss Desmond?"

"Yes—of course."

"You'll look at the body?"

"Yes, Sergeant Morris—of course—"

CHAPTER 11

The waiter at Blancharde's leaned morosely against the bar, and morosely studied a copy of the *Gazette*. His sad eyes snailed across the picture of Clara Davis and then went back to it.

He said to the bartender: "I've got a feeling I've seen this dame before."

The bartender looked.

"In here? She isn't one of the regulars."

"Maybe not in here, but somewhere. It feels like I've seen her a couple of times."

"And what's so remarkable about that?"

The waiter shoved the paper away and said: "Nothing. Give me a beer."

He drank the beer, pulling the paper back again and reading the story. It nagged him. The story in itself was flossy—one meant, after all! A socialite of the town in rushes, with herself in nothing. Idly his mind (sic) revolved. That face. Not that it mattered. Not that anything ever mattered—but that face—faces?

"I'm going to the funeral," he said.

"What funeral?" the bartender said, slicing his groceries for the old-fashioned's trade.

"Her's. They show them off."

"They what?"

"Parade. People walk around and look into the coffin. Last respects. I want to look at her again."

"And even so?"

"Because," the waiter said carefully, being already half-seas over, "I've got that notion I've seen her twice. And I don't mean any pink elephants."

"Tricks, now."

"No, and no illusions. Irregardless."

"That," the bartender said decisively, "is no such word. Not in any dictionary."

The waiter became a bit elegant. "People talked," he said, "before there were dictionaries."

"Rudolph, you've got something there."

"It's the trouble with now. Guys—Websters—Emily Posts—that bunch of helium-inflated big brains in Washington—tell you when to change your shirts—rats—shove over another beer."

That face.

CHAPTER 12

Night fell and Mrs. Lovestone, finished with supper—jellied eel, smoked carp, awfully good sour-rye bread, and three chocolate éclairs from Johnson's, the perfect meal for a hot night en-dressing-gown, with pepsi—settled down in her living room, and checked her advertisement in the evening edition of the *Gazette*.

Below her the vacant apartment, cleaned and in shape—the breezy Mr. Suffern had simply not cared, in and out, one of those things—waited. Even though it was evening Mrs. Lovestone waited too: either for the street door buzzer or for the telephone bell.

It was a lonesome life, really, being an apartment house keeper, when the apartments were segments of your own home, which you had lived in with Albert. Albert hadn't been romantic, it was true, but even without his non-extended little finger, he had been warm and lovably human, someone near her, with her, and she did miss him. She missed the absence. The vacuum left by the loneliness of his no longer being, in his virile, hairy way, around.

Because it was such a lonesome life—it wasn't that she didn't have friends, because she did have, but it was her house, her *home* which was empty without Albert—she had to occupy her mind with her tenants who really didn't mean a thing, warmly, humanly, to her.

She continued to bemuse herself with the accidental drowning of Clara Davis and its attendant coincidences of looks and time with Solda Carmandine.

Actually there was no decisive significance in the affair for Mrs. Lovestone, beyond it being something to mull over that was more exciting than the usual run of her mullings—cigarette holes in the furnished apartments, burns and scars on surfaces, all the general run of headaches besetting an owner. She kept worrying it, with the tenacious gentleness of a cat's preliminary pats upon a fresh-caught mouse.

The telephone rang.

"This is the Lovestone Apartments," she said in the special voice she reserved for such announcements. It was a mélange of ultra-social and briskly businesslike.

"Mrs. Lovestone?"

"Yes, this," (in the ultra-social), "is she speaking."

"This," the woman's voice said, "is Solda Carmandine."

Mrs. Lovestone was flabbergasted, and prickles settled along her spine.

"But I've been thinking about you, Miss Carmandine—thinking about you all day."

"I'm telephoning from the restaurant in the station. I've just got in from Philadelphia, Mrs. Lovestone, and I saw your advertisement in the *Gazette*. Am I still in time?"

Mrs. Lovestone continued to feel the needling thrill of this oddest of all the coincidences.

"Time?" she said stupidly.

"Is the apartment still open? May I rent it?"

"Oh of course, Miss Carmandine, and it's the *same* one that you had before."

"I'll bring my things right out, if I may?"

"By all means." Mrs. Lovestone's voice shook loose from its fluttering, and became more solid. "I shall want to hear all about it."

"Oh—?" The pause held for a lengthening moment over the wire. "Oh yes, the vacation—and what I'm afraid was my terribly rude departure."

Mrs. Lovestone accepted this as a complete amende. "Miss Carmandine, I sort of guessed," she said with a roguish touch.

"Guessed—what, Mrs. Lovestone?"

"Wasn't it a man?"

There was a further pause at the other end of the line, one which Mrs. Lovestone easily attributed to a proper splash of maidenly confusion.

"Yes," the woman's voice said, "It was a man. I'll be there in about half an hour, Mrs. Lovestone."

Mrs. Lovestone, vicariously bathed in a haze of the pinkest romance, hung up. Solda Carmandine's voice had sounded a bit keener than she recalled it. It had always been sort of slow-flowing, lazy. But voices over the telephone sometimes gave that effect, and until now they had never spoken with each other over the telephone.

She felt something special about this, about Miss Carmandine coming back—popping back, really—on the button of that remarkable resemblance between her and the unhappily, thoroughly drowned socialite Mrs. Harold Davis. In a fashion it seemed to call for something. Mrs. Lovestone changed from negligee into a summer dress (polka-dot), hatted herself and went out.

At Felicio's, on the nearby corner of Wagburn Street, she bought some early asters—a bunch of the almost-pink ones—then went back and opened up Solda's rooms, putting the asters in a souvenir, and horrible, vase from Atlantic City where she and Albert had spent their honeymoon, because Albert had decided to be original, and not to go to Niagara Falls.

Miss Carmandine won't be here long, Mrs. Lovestone decided. Thinking of her "threes."

CHAPTER 13

The railroad station restaurant at Blush Falls was a fair-sized room, with a lunch counter and a reasonable amount of table service. This was indifferently handled by two young women who were, nevertheless, old enough to be thoroughly down on life. Their concerted reaction to lone female diners was negative, almost to the point of blindness.

Mae absently checked the fact that the woman who got up from her table, and headed for the telephone booths, had left her coat across the back of the chair, and the veal cutlet blue-plate unfinished. Contrary to established precedent, Mae had found herself looking twice at the woman, and almost actually seeing her.

Clara replaced the receiver on its hook. She felt agreeably reassured. Her voice, which she had cadenced to the homely middle-west tones which had been Solda Carmandine's, had apparently gone over very well with Mrs. Lovestone. She walked back to her table, and took up where she had left off with the veal cutlet blue plate.

Clara was completely at ease. She felt her plans to be as orderly as a fresh deck of cards. Nothing had gone wrong. Nothing whatever.

There were no intricacies to attend to. Her traveling suit and hat had been Solda's best, as were the mediocre handbag and washable gloves. Her hairdo was of a simple homemade variety that would have driven her own hairdresser, through pained pallor, into a decline—this being Edmonde who had tried and succeeded in giving her, in his tough way, a reasonable facsimile of—on her Blush Falls formal appearances—a touch of the Marquise de Maintenon, that lacquer which had interested Louis XIV.

Her fingernails were trimmed short in the fashion which Solda had found essential for typing, and were bloody with the predatory shade which Solda had favored—predatory in the sense of translating a woman's fingernails into claws.

Solda's wardrobe had not been an extensive one. It now rested in two suitcases, with Solda's portable radio, in the checkroom at the door. There had been very few fripperies about Solda, and they certainly had not extended to overnight bags, makeup kits, or jewel cases.

Clara ended her meal with maple-walnut ice cream and coffee. She paid the check, and went into the women's room where she took an inch-wide roll of medical gauze from the handbag and, with an adroit stab at clumsiness, bandaged the index finger of her right hand, cutting the gauze with a nail scissors and knotting it about her wrist with her teeth. The room, except for herself, was empty.

She handed the baggage check to a porter and asked him to get her a taxi. She gave the driver Mrs. Lovestone's address on Ashcourt Street, then settled back to steep herself in the role of Solda as she had determined it during the hours when they had been together.

Clara appreciated and accepted the risk she was about to face. She accepted it because it was essential. Her picture in the *Gazette* had made an appearance in the flesh as Solda Carmandine, before Mrs. Lovestone's eyes, seem to be imperative.

She had gleaned from Solda that Mrs. Lovestone had an insatiable aptitude for mulling, and furthermore for being activated about it. Nothing but a personal appearance would erase with finality the co-incidental features of the Davis case from Mrs. Lovestone's revolving mind.

It was reassuring that Solda's passion for privacy had been unique. It was equally reassuring that the house on Ashcourt Street was completely remote from the milieu of her life with Harold, or that of Harold's friends.

Curious that Mrs. Lovestone should have selected a man as having been the motivation for Solda's peremptory departure—a man, with Mrs. Lovestone's unsubtle overtones of a breathless romance, and an elderly syrup of love-at-first-sight. Yes, Clara decided, this was palpably what Mrs. Lovestone expected, so this was certainly what Mrs. Lovestone would get.

Mentally the man took shape: a touch of premature gray to lend his virile, dark hair a distinguished look, the solidity and large bank account of some forty-odd years, years, whose mark had not effaced a certain—rapturous? Too thick? No, not for Mrs. Lovestone would it be too thick—a certain rapturous quality of youth. In brief, the most vital sort of masculinity gloved in a considerate and tender suede.

So far so good, but where was he? And what did he do to keep him (as he certainly would have to be) apart from his betrothed? All right, he was en route to South America, a mining engineer, sleuthing for gold—nitrates?—copper? Oh by all means gold. In the Andes, with a forwarding address in Lima, Peru.

Having settled her fiancé, Clara felt fine. It was extraordinary how she had continued to feel perfectly fine throughout the past week. There had been no mental horrors in the dark of night—no remorse—no dreading the clammy embrace of a fearful retribution—no nerve-shaking fear at an ultimate discovery of her horrendous crime.

Well, almost none—

The cab stopped.

"We're here, lady," the driver said.

CHAPTER 14

Clara's feeling of fineness wore thin almost from the start of a nervous hour she was compelled to suffer with Mrs. Lovestone, in the small apartment which once had been Solda Carmandine's.

The nondescript dullness of the place abetted an approach to a crisis of nerves. Its lamps were shaded in a manner strongly advertised to diffuse a genteel glow, which settled with a melancholic apology on mustard-colored walls, sparsely spotted with sub-moronic prints in gilt frames.

The furnishings were dismal, while the two windows of the living room were muffled in auction-sale draperies of a mulberry hue. Outside these windows a rush of minor litter along Ashcourt Street gave gloomy promise of an impending summer storm.

Mrs. Lovestone herself was in keeping with the mise en scène. After the first flurry of greetings, the presentation, and the thanks for the asters, she was concerned about her tenant's bandaged finger. She fussed, and then kept right on fussing, with that poisonous determination of a person who insists on being helpful.

She put away the contents of the two suitcases ("No, Miss Carmandine, I refuse to let you touch a thing. I remember perfectly where you kept things."), racked the modest wardrobe, and plugged the portable radio into what had been its accustomed place.

In one way, and in spite of her nervous irritation, Clara was glad of this bravura performance. Seeing and handling all the possessions which had been Solda's would quench in Mrs. Lovestone's mind any least flicker of doubt concerning Clara's impersonation.

The job ended, Mrs. Lovestone selected a chair close to Clara's and sat down.

"Now then," she said, "we can talk. Miss Carmandine, you have no idea how glad I am to see you back. To know you are safe."

"Safe? But didn't you get my note?"

"No, there was nothing in the envelope but your key and the rent, and your Arabian departure."

"My—what?"

"Tents. Folding them and stealing away."

"Oh, of course."

"In the night."

"Mrs. Lovestone, how stupid of me! I can remember just what I had meant to write—only Robert—"

Clara permitted the sentence, with its implication of a man's lover-like impatience, to trail away, while taking a fresh grip on her depleting nerves.

"So that's his name, Robert who, Miss Carmandine?"

"Robert Johnson."

"You won't mind my asking—but when are the nuptials to be?"

Clara launched into the script which she had prepared in the cab. The wedding would be when Robert returned from South America. Being a mining engineer, as well as having several rich holdings of his own, he had had to fly to Peru to inspect a gold mine in the Andes, a task which might hold him there for months, possibly even a year.

"Oh, but my dear Miss Carmandine, how can you bear the separation?"

"It isn't easy, Mrs. Lovestone. I would have gone with Robert, only he said I never could stand the hardships of the camps."

"I should say not." Mrs. Lovestone, whose knowledge of life in the Andes was far from complete, added: "Wild men and wilder beasts."

"Robert had all sorts of thoughtful suggestions about where I ought to stay while waiting his return."

"I should think his family—"

"No, his parents have been dead for years and the family estate's been sold for ever so long, and, of course, his own bachelor ménage would be out of the question."

"Well, I should say it would be. After all!"

Clara herself had decided on returning to Blush Falls where she (Solda) had spent the few happy years since having left home in Bethel. Robert—Mrs. Lovestone would surely understand this if she knew his nature, the nobility of his nature—had insisted on arranging with his bankers to open quite a large account in her name.

The ice grew a little thin. Mrs. Lovestone would also in her kindness understand that the stay in the apartment would only be temporary, until a house could be leased. Robert had put his expensive foot down firmly about this—there must be a house and servants for his fiancée's very own.

"Miss Carmandine, I understand completely. It would have astonished me had a man of Mr. Johnson's position and wealth permitted anything less." Mrs. Lovestone, at long last, stood up. "My dear, I can see that you are tired."

"I am, Mrs. Lovestone, very."

Mrs. Lovestone pondered the appropriateness of a good mutual mulling over at this moment of the Mrs. Harold Davis drowning, with its interesting set of coincidences. She decided not. It would remove the bloom from her tenant's homecoming.

"You're to get a good night's rest," she said, "and not to think of a thing. I'll tell the milkman, in the morning, that you're back, and he'll leave the usual. And by the way, Miss Carmandine, you owe him for the last week you were here."

"Oh how careless of me!"

"One dollar and eighty-five cents. I did try to get a forwarding address from your father but so far there has been no reply."

Clara tensed.

"You wrote to—Bethel, Mrs. Lovestone?"

"I do hope you don't mind, but the milkman was just a bit upset. I wonder—I mean I did just mention to your father the, well, the suddenness of your leaving—I do wonder whether you oughtn't to drop him a card?"

"What was it you did tell him, Mrs. Lovestone?"

"Why—everything, dear, and in my second little letter about the drowning—I mean that poor unfortunate Mrs. Davis looked so much like you, and the same day and everything."

Clara felt her skin chilling to ice.

"Would you tell me all about this, please? Exactly all about it?"

Mrs. Lovestone did while Clara's nerves lost some of their tension. It was mutually agreed upon that such startling resemblances did exist. So often one said to a friend: My dear, you're the image of Constance Bennett, you ought to be in the movies.

Just the same, Mrs. Lovestone still felt, Mr. Carmandine should be written to. In an excess of zeal to be helpful to her now wealthy tenant Mrs. Lovestone announced that she herself would drop a line and explain that Miss Carmandine was unable to do so personally because of her poor injured and bandaged finger.

"No—no, Miss Carmandine, I really insist. It will be no trouble at all. I'll get it off the first thing in the morning. And now, good night."

The door closed.

CHAPTER 15

The glum apartment, the storm's first rumble of thunder, closed in on Clara. She went to bed and slept fitfully for several hours. She awoke at three in the strange darkness. An unreasoning upsurge of fear caused her swiftly, almost with panic, to turn on the bed lamp.

Nothing even remotely frightening was in the room. Nothing was there beyond its weary furniture—except for the meager and unimportant little treasures which had been Solda's.

But sleep was gone and, through the careful locks of memory, Solda came in sleep's place.

"What a lovely camp, Clara—"

"Harold designed it. It's nice in winter, too, with the fire going and snow on the ground—"

"Oh I can just see it! What do you call it—"

"The camp? Why nothing."

"I thought they always had names, like Woody Nook, or—oh, you know—"

"Indeed I do know—"

Later:

"This salad is delicious, Clara. My but I'm glad we met, and that you thought of coming out here. Tell me, do you believe in fate—"

"Yes, I believe in Fate—"

"Mama always did, too. She had so many stories—"

Later: "But isn't it dangerous to swim at night, Clara?—"

"Of course it isn't. If we hadn't spent the afternoon talking—"

"Honest, I don't remember ever telling anybody so much about myself. I guess there isn't a single thing you don't know—"

"Let's change to swim suits. It will be full moonlight soon—"

But not light enough for eyes to see, as no eyes had seen the two of them together, secluded in the camp house through the late afternoon and the pale twilight hours.

"Is the water very deep, Clara—"

"No, it's shallow right here, and gradual. There's no current to speak of. Take my hand—"

And then after a while:

"You're sure I won't sink—"

"Just lie flat on your back and breathe easily. My hand will be under you—"

"Why, it's lovely. Like floating on air—

"Clara!—

"*Clara*—

"Cla…"

CHAPTER 16

The inquest, which was brief and completely cut-and-dried, had small effect on Harold's nervous system, whereas the funeral upset it very much. In addition to the emotionally upsetting rituals of church and cemetery services, there were the groups of morbidly curious strangers who regularly form an insufferable band of camp followers on the fringe of a publicized tragedy.

Also, to a man and woman, there were Harold's friends. With the kindest intentions in the world they had staunchly bulwarked him, overmuch so when you came right down to it. Almost there was an undercurrent of welcoming him home, fully home again within their fold, as though he had been absent or, if this were possible, not entirely there.

It had dawned on Harold with a cumulative force that this semi-absent period must have been the duration of his marriage with Clara—now so publicly being terminated with the hot wax of banked candles, the funereal pungency of over-massed flowers, packed bodies, and the self-indulgent tears of totally strange females.

Especially difficult were the decorous gestures of his friends which spilled over, now that Clara was out of the picture, into a scarcely concealed determination to take him—poor, happily lonely fellow—in hand. He must not brood, and above all else he must not be alone. Such was the gist of it. It even progressed to several kindlily plotting eyes resting speculatively on Edna Washburton, and then turning almost fixedly back upon Harold.

Following the service, in the main portion of the church, the casket was wheeled into a small chapel where, before being sealed, friends could take their farewell look. A truly remarkable job had been done and Solda, in a fashionable hairdo and white satin dress, looked more the image of Clara than ever.

Fifi Desmond hesitated somewhat longer than most and looked at the calm, waxen face more sharply. That police officer (Sergeant Morris?) having asked her out at her house whether she planned to do so—well, it had slightly puzzled and bothered her. It seemed meaningless now. This was Clara.

The bartender from Blanchardes, neatly and morbidly dressed in a dark purplish blue serge, looked too. Sure, he knew that face. And still—where?

Mrs. Lovestone paused and dropped a few polite tears, elegantly stemming them with a handkerchief bordered with Brussel's lace, which Albert had picked up from a merchant seaman, and given her on a birthday. She did so wish that Miss Carmandine were here too, instead of being back at the apartment with an announced splitting headache.

The spotlight next turned to the grave, and it was over.

Edna left the cemetery with Harold, and Patterson drove them along the country club road at the sedate pace which he considered correct for a departure from a funeral. The sun was already masked behind outlying hills, while the western sky had softened to the pistache tones of evening.

"Have dinner with me tonight, Harold," Edna said.

"I'd like to, Edna. But I won't, if you don't mind."

"Of course I don't mind."

"I feel—I don't know just what I do feel, Edna. I think I may have some tea and go right to bed."

"Do that, Harold."

The solitary cortege continued, under Patterson's sedate throttle, on its way. The Athertons' place, with its stunning rows of Lombardy poplars, flowed quietly by. The Wycherlys, and its groupings of Koster blue spruce.

Harold said: "I didn't tell you."

"Tell me what?"

"About that policeman, Sergeant Morris. He spoke with me just as we were breaking up to go to the cars. He only offered me his sympathies. He was very correctly conventional about it, but I had a feeling that it meant something."

"I don't see why?"

"Well, I mean it was funny his even being there. Why should he have been? Surely his job must keep him pretty well occupied. Clara meant nothing to him."

"Please, Harold—please, dear—don't go on letting things worry you. It's over with. Truly it is."

"Yes, I suppose you're right."

CHAPTER 17

Mrs. Lovestone reread her latest communication to her unresponsive correspondent.

Dear Mr. Carmandine,

You will be delighted to know that your daughter has returned to her dear little nest, so that no more need be said about the milk bill. She would, I am sure, have written you herself but an injury to her hand makes it awkward for her to hold a pen.

She has *such* exciting news to tell you as soon as her hand is better. I do not feel privileged more than to give you the tiniest hint of the happiness and fortune which will be hers before another year is out—in fact, a goodly portion of its wealth is even hers right now. As I often say, dear Mr. Carmandine, some people are simply born to *luck*.

Very truly yours,

ADELIA LOVESTONE

Mrs. Lovestone addressed the envelope and stamped it. It had been a busy day. Her tenants in Number 9 had overflowed the tub, with the result that a sizeable piece of plaster in Number 7 below had fallen, and both messes had had to be attended to, including a lengthy soothing of Number 7 because of the plasterized lunch.

Then the funeral had taken up the afternoon, with its wonderful flowers, and organ music, and crush, and that poor, dear woman in white satin so still, so away from it all. Well on the whole it had not been until now that she had been able to fulfill her promise and write to Mr. Carmandine.

A cupid clock on the mantel informed her that the hour was approaching nine. A pleasant evening had erased the heat of day, and a cool breeze came gently through the open windows. She leaned back in the chair for a moment of delicious rest.

The clock struck.

Several minutes passed before Mrs. Lovestone began to feel that something was wrong. Not wrong exactly, but rather out of place. She set about pinning it down. The faint infiltration of Solda Carmandine's radio was coming through the floor, just as it always had on the nights after nights during her previous occupancy.

But—

Mrs. Lovestone looked at the clock. Yes, it *was* nine—but the program, faintly heard from below, was the impassioned jazz diddling and doodling of a well known band. What ever on earth! *Never* had Miss Carmandine previously deviated from dialing in *The Tale of Lost Loves* hour. Until now.

Instantly Mrs. Lovestone mulled. She ran the gamut of How-odds! How-queers! Then she pulled herself together. It was quite simple, really—it was just another result of the wealthy and romantic Mr. Johnson. Full happiness had flooded the empty and lonesome well of dreams. Miss Carmandine's need for the poignancy of that program, with its solace for all women who were alone, was gone.

Her love had come.

Mrs. Lovestone, not feeling even remotely like one of the Parcae, went out and posted her letter in the corner box. No thunder rolled, nor did the heavens split. The calm night remained simply pleasant and cool.

She returned to her rooms and, putting her once-titian hair in curlers, went to bed.

CHAPTER 18

The morning which followed the funeral was bright with sun. For the first time in any number of days Harold felt thoroughly rested. He made a most leisurely toilet, one utterly lacking in the anxious super-niceties he had rigidly adhered to during his attempts at pace with Clara.

His shaving was once-over only, and that all down. His eyes received no drops, his hair no brilliantine. He allowed his stomach to plump out as comfortably as it liked, discarding, with a sigh of pleased finality, the moderate aid-to-grooming which he had been accustomed to snap around his middle.

He found himself almost running down the stairs, and telling Effie, now in her active sixties, that he thought he would have two eggs for breakfast instead of the usual one. Even the garden seemed less frowsy than it had for the past couple of years.

He discovered and picked a rose, placing it in the buttonhole of his jacket. Possibly Edna could help him find somebody to put the place back in shape. How wonderful were her roses, everything about her house, about herself. A fine, fine woman. In the very essences that his mother had been fine.

He not only ate a good breakfast, but enjoyed it. Effie waited until he had finished, and then produced her cloud.

"Mr. Harold, just what would you care to have Agnes and me do about Mrs. Davis's things?"

It brought Clara back at once, fracturing the tranquility of the moment. She was all there again, still in the house. Was it like that? Would she always be?

"Effie, I don't know. I suppose if they were just put away?"

"It's customary for them to be got rid of, Mr. Harold." The idea seemed brutally realistic. Cruel, too. It was a big house and surely there were places where they could be kept.

"It's morbid not to, Mr. Harold," Effie said. "And really it's always done."

"Let me think about it, Effie. I'll let you know."

"All right, Mr. Harold."

Around ten o'clock he called up Edna.

"It's about Clara's things," he said. "You know—her clothes, Edna, all of her things. Effie says they ought to be got rid of, that that's what's done. Edna, it doesn't seem kind. I thought you'd know."

"Effie's right, Harold. It's always a hard thing to face, but truly it's morbid not to. And it doesn't mean throwing them away, or burning them—nothing like that."

"It doesn't?"

"No, Harold. Usually they're given to the Red Cross or to some fine organization where they'll be, in turn, given to people who need them—sometimes need them desperately, Harold."

"That's different. That seems all right, doesn't it, Edna?"

"It is absolutely all right. Shall I come over and help?"

"Would you, Edna?"

"I'll go over now.

She came very shortly and, with Effie's assistance, assembled suits, dresses, underwear, the whole accumulation of Clara's possessions and arranged them in proper bundles. After a few fumbling and rejected gestures at helping, Harold just moved around and watched.

It was friendly having Edna there, intimate in an almost family sense. He had the oddest impression that it was like having his mother about again—her dignity—quietness—her assured authority. The change in Effie struck him as remarkable. She was more as she had used to be in the bygone years, much more the real old Effie. As if she were back in some satisfying groove from which she had for a while been jolted.

"What shall we do about the jewelry, Harold?"

"Well, a good deal of it was Mother's. We might as well put all of it away at the bank, I suppose. Have you come across a locket?"

"No. What kind?"

"A silly thing. Its only value is sentimental, and I'd rather like to keep it around. Possibly you remember Mother wearing it, Edna? There are two small rounds of glass with a clip of my hair between them. They're set in a gold ring."

Edna thought back and she did remember it, and most vividly remembered Mrs. Davis.

"You gave that to Clara?" she asked, and could at once have bitten her tongue out for having done so.

"Yes, I did." Harold felt his face flushing. "It's funny, Edna, how completely overboard you can go about a person. There's no limit to it really. Do you suppose it's usually just a form of self-delusion? Sort of a blind projection of one's self?"

"No, Harold, not always."

"Well, possibly not."

Edna and Effie looked everywhere, but there was no little locket with its clip of baby's hair.

"Please don't bother, Edna. It's absurd to think that Clara could have had it with her, and it can't be lost." He was standing at a window watching a cloud encroach and then blot out the brilliance of the sun.

He said: "It's bound to show up."

CHAPTER 19

The locket on its long slender chain had never been absent from Clara. She had worn it night and day from the moment when her plan, on that Thursday, had meshed into its machinelike action. The camp business done, with its conveniently simple completion of Solda, it had been necessary to risk a return to the house during the earlier hours of the night before Harold would have returned.

Actually she had felt, and as there was not, there would not be any risk. She had her key, and Effie and Agnes were always profound in their sleep. She had stolen through its dark quietness to her rooms, and taken from their place of concealment behind some books on a shelf, certain papers which she wanted, and a bank book.

It would be folly, even though the desire was almost irresistible, to take any of the jewels but she could not resist a last look. Strangely, it was the insignificant little locket which had held her more than any of them. It had lifted vividly from her memory the stanza when Enoch Arden, in a positive lather of what Clara had dubbed mawkish sentimentality, had taken farewell of his wife, his babes, his home.

> *But Annie from her baby's forehead clipt*
> *A tiny curl, and gave it; this he kept*
> *Thro' all his future, ...*

Surely this was a sign! Every known and unknown superstition in her—and heaven knows there were plenty—had compelled her to take the locket: a talisman so pregnantly offered her by Fate.

Clara fingered it now while sitting in the rakish roadster which Mr. Artemus Simms (real estate—be it Walkup or Palace it's a Home) used when selling his more youthful prospects. For the decrepit set he employed a respectful sedan.

"Just about a mile more now, Miss Carmandine. Perfect for the seclusion you're looking for, and still ideally convenient to town. You'll keep a car, of course?"

"Naturally, Mr. Simms."

"May have a bit of trouble keeping servants until you weed out the jitterbug addicts—of course you could always chain them down."

Mr. Simms ha-ha-ha'd and Clara laughed politely too. She observed with satisfaction the stretches of wasteland, then the patches of scrub forest through which they were passing (rakishly) in this purlieu of the town which had never been built up. No one but an idiot would live out here. Even a hermit would view the setup with alarm.

The house itself, when they came to it, was of convenient size and good colonial architecture. It sat in a reasonably sized clearing among a forest of pines. A separate building held a garage with an apartment above it for a chauffeur. The house itself seemed, and was on more detailed inspection, in excellent repair.

"Why on earth did Mr. Watertown ever leave it?" Clara asked.

"He went West."

This was Mr. Simms's private little joke. He told it to all the prospects who would come for a look, then shudder at the environment, and go away. Mr. Watertown had gone West all right, in the sense that the expression had been used during World War I. His body, in a state of no preservation whatsoever, had eventually been discovered suspended by a piece of clothesline from an attic rafter early last fall. A suicide note had been illegibly scrawled, except for the word "depressed."

"When can I take possession?" Clara asked.

Mr. Simms almost literally rocked back on his heels.

"You come straight back to the office with me, Miss Carmandine, and the place is yours as of right now."

The lease was a standard form and ran for a year. It included the usual exacting trivia—damage to furniture, breakage, loss and so forth— and Clara signed it without reading it, or question.

Mr. Simms continued to feel overcome. He said, in this flush of flabbergasted gratitude at getting the Watertown white elephant off his hands: "You'll need a man out there, Miss Carmandine."

"I know I will, Mr. Simms."

"I might be able to help you, if you liked."

"I'd appreciate it very much."

"He's strong, and he drives. Incidentally, he has a car of his own. Perhaps you might care to make some arrangement with him about its use until your own comes through?"

"I would be glad to."

"I'll give him a ring. When would it be convenient for you to see him?"

"This afternoon? Around five?"

"Fine. I'll give him your address. His name is Joe."

"Just Joe?"

"He has a last one, of course, but nobody has ever been able to pronounce it—one of those things that are all consonants and only one vowel. He's of some middle-European stock. I'd settle for just Joe, Miss Carmandine."

"All right, I will."

Clara thanked Mr. Simms and said good-by. It was a little before one o'clock, and she went into an obscure tea room off the shopping center, and ordered a light lunch. She felt the imperative necessity for buying some new clothes. It was curious how the physical touch of Solda's things was beginning to affect her.

She had not been conscious of this before that inexplicable moment of fright which she had felt last night, with its aftermath of sleeplessness and memory. She ate tomato salad, and wondered whether there could be anything in the notion: could something of a person be left in his belongings after he was dead?

Clara avoided the better shops where she had been known, and managed to assemble a fairly good collection at the lesser ones, paying cash for her purchases and having them sent to Ashcourt Street.

It occurred to her that it would be expedient to buy a present for Mrs. Lovestone. A Solda, suddenly wrapped in wealth and romance, would certainly have done so. She carefully considered Mrs. Lovestone.

Fur.

Clara felt herself safe here because her own furs had always been bought in New York. She went to the better of the only two shops in Blush Falls that handled them, and shortly settled on a very good silver fox, paying cash for it, and saying she would take it with her. It was a quiet, small store and almost distinctively elegant in its way. It had the hush about it. Subdued lighting. So far she had been the sole customer.

A woman came in as she was leaving it, and Clara realized with a nerve-wrenching shock that the woman was Ethel Manlow, a reasonably intimate friend of Harold's and of herself.

Clara did not falter. She was still dressed in Solda's mediocre clothes and bargain-counter hat with, under it, Solda's plain hairdo. She did not hesitate for an instant. She walked straight past Ethel Manlow, but not so rapidly that she failed to catch a glance of the look which settled like swift cement on Mrs. Manlow's face.

The sort of look you say people would have if they had seen a ghost.

Once on the street, and in a taxicab, Clara felt shaken. She decided against going around town again without some slight disguise. Even sun glasses, obvious though they were, would do.

With an uncanny sort of exactitude the bell of her apartment rang precisely at five. Clara opened the door, and the man standing in the hallway said: "Miss Carmandine? I'm Joe."

He was a big man, young, and in the light of the living room Clara got a better look at him. His hair was dark, as were his eyes, and heightened the contrast with his skin which was very smooth, the color of pale alabaster.

There was nothing unhealthy about its look. There couldn't be, because his whole body radiated an almost bursting sense of strength and of vitality. He held himself with the quiet, assured poise of a professional athlete. His smile added the final touch of good looks to his face.

"Let's sit down, Joe," Clara said.

CHAPTER 20

Evening fell, and in the Manlow house a handsome Georgian place in Fortley Square, Ethel and Britton Manlow sat down to dinner.

Ethel said, in the middle of an entree of cold duck with broiled mushrooms and asparagus: "I don't believe in ghosts, dear. I suppose nobody truly does. You don't, do you, Britton?"

Britton, who was replaying the seventh hole, as well as eating heartily, said: "Yes."

"You *do*?"

"I do what, Ethel?"

"Ghosts—believe in them?"

"Certainly I don't. Why?"

"Because I could have sworn I ran into Clara Davis in the Burton Fur Shop this afternoon."

"Nonsense. She's dead."

"I *know*, dear—"

"We went to her funeral yesterday afternoon. Remember?"

"I know, dear—"

"Most interminable thing I ever was at in my life. I think I'll stipulate having mine twice as long, just to get even."

"Britton, do listen—this woman I saw was the living image of Clara Davis."

"Suppose she was? Lots of people look alike. Especially women."

"It wasn't only the looks—I don't know how to say this, but there was that *feeling* that passed between us."

"Well you don't say it very clearly."

"Electric—no, psychical—honestly it shocked me so that you could almost call it grave-like."

"Go right ahead and call it grave-like. Did you speak to her—although I believe the proper term is communicate?"

"Of course not. Anyhow, she just went right by and out into the street."

"What on earth would you expect her to do? Dissolve?"

"Oh really, Britton—I—this will seem positively crazy, but I had the strongest impulse to call up Harold."

"Ethel, in the good name of common sense, why?"

"Well, when you consider her death, the strangeness of it—"

"She got a cramp and drowned. Her lungs were full of water. Happens every day."

"But it was violent and, oh you know the old wives' tales—surely England is full of them, the castles, and walkings at night."

"This wasn't at night. According to you it was full afternoon, and not in a castle, but in a fur shop. Forget it.

"I will, of course, and it does seem sort of silly now."

"And for heaven's sake don't go calling up Harold."

"I won't."

"Ring for some more asparagus, will you?"

* * * *

A little later that evening, while she sat in her chair, Mrs. Lovestone wore the silver fox even though the air drifting in through the windows was humid and warm.

She stroked the fur's lustrous richness ceaselessly, while she cried.

Except for this wonderful, generous gesture of Miss Carmandine's no one since Albert had ever done anything spontaneously kind to her, and even Albert hadn't gone in for it very much, really just when there were bargains.

She wanted ever so hard to do something for Miss Carmandine to repay her for making herself feel, well, important again, as if she truly meant something to somebody. To somebody who cared. And it *was* hard, because as Mrs. Lovestone always said, what could you give a person who already had everything?

A somewhat staggeringly happy thought came. Miss Carmandine, with her new house, would need a housekeeper, and servants were very hard to get. Not that with Miss Carmandine there would be any question about wages, but a good servant, one whom she could trust. With the further happy comfort of killing two birds with one stone, Mrs. Lovestone instantly thought of her friend Mrs. Porter. Ideal for both of them.

And furthermore Mrs. Porter could act as a sort of friendly thread of liaison between Miss Carmandine's new milieu and her old.

* * * *

The moon swung high, and Morris still sat at his desk. The daily routine of his job had been completed. He had interviewed the usual spatter of harassed, grief-stricken, and distracted people. He had studied, with more than his accustomed interest, all the reports that came in, not only the local ones but from those of the surrounding and the distant states as well.

With the infinite patience of the police he had done this for days, just sat there and waited. There was something of the spider about him.

Yesterday afternoon, at the funeral, a faint ripple along his nerves had hinted that some breaks might come. That morose man, in the purplish blue serge suit, who had joined the procession of the more intimate friends around the coffin in the smaller chapel. The man hadn't been an idle curiosity seeker. Normally he wasn't the type who would have been caught dead at any funeral other than his own. No, he had gone there with a purpose.

Morris glanced at his notes. Rudolph Schilling, a waiter at Blancharde's where Morris had followed him. So far there was nothing out of him beyond the fact that he'd seen that face, Clara Davis's face, twice. This interested Morris very much. He intended to see Rudolph again and, if necessary, again.

That woman who had looked too. She hadn't belonged. The one wearing her "best" dress and, for God's sake, that hat. The tears and the handkerchief with the border of Brussel's lace. Both had seemed genuine. Morris wished he could have followed her too, but the man at the time had seemed more important.

Well, he'd find her.

The last note he had jotted down had been from the death certificate. Clara Davis's maiden name had been Malden. It was a note, but at least, out of the utter blank of her past, it was something to know.

He called up his wife, Freda.

"I'm coming home now," he said.

CHAPTER 21

A Minnesota sun scorched hotly on parched fields, and coursed the sweat in tricklets from Antonio Carmandine's brutish brow down the chunk of his short neck, and bathed the power of his butternut-browned torso with a Vaseline glow. He gathered the morning's mail from the roadside box, and retreated with it to the negligent shade of the front porch.

Again he left the letter, from that gibbering pest in Blush Falls, until the last. For two cents, for one cent, he would have torn up the envelope and letter, unopened and unread.

Constitutionally, however, it was impossible for him to do this with any communication whatever which came to him through the mails. He was in a smoldering rage to begin with (eighteen of his pullets had died during the night, of some fantastic virus that could not be localized) and he masochistically decided to torture himself still further by reading the senile, superannuated, doddering creature's drip.

He read Mrs. Lovestone's effusion through and then, more carefully, he read it again.

His self-styled keenly analytical mind cudded tidbits from its phrases: *Exciting news—happiness and fortune—portion of its wealth—now—luck—*

What precisely was it the old fossil meant? In meditative succession his superlative deductions ruminated through lotteries, sweepstakes, baseball pools, the numbers. By the time he had reached the possibility that some moonstruck octogenarian (either sex) had died, and in a final fit of utter madness had bequeathed Solda a fortune, Carmandine truly was fit to be tied.

His rage shifted from smoldering to flash-pan, while he shredded the letter with enough force to have bent a crowbar, letting the pieces drift through the listless air down on the porch floor.

He returned to his work.

About an hour later Carmandine steamed back to the house.

He said to his fat housekeeper: "Olga, where are those bits of paper that were on the porch?"

"They are with the rest of the rubbish, Tony."

"Burned?"

"No, not yet."

"Find them, Olga. I want each one."

CHAPTER 22

Clara settled into her new home.

In addition to Joe and his car she had Mrs. Porter. Mrs. Porter was the present from Mrs. Lovestone in return for the silver fox. Both women had, for years, been friends, but whereas Mrs. Lovestone eked a satisfactory enough living from her tenants, Mrs. Porter was in circumstances so reduced that it was silly to call them circumstances at all. Furthermore, according to her own and Mrs. Lovestone's pronouncements, she was a lady.

The gift had been bestowed during a coffee session *bien haut monde* on the day of her departure from Solda's apartment, and Clara (she would have selected almost any other type of housekeeper for the close confinement of the indeterminate future) found herself saddled with Mrs. Porter, whose spindle body and flat face habitually imparted an aura which barely missed the moribund.

Clara had taken practically nothing, except her new purchases, to the house in the pines. She had left Solda's trifling wardrobe to be disposed of, as Mrs. Lovestone wished, and had insisted upon Mrs. Lovestone accepting the portable radio.

The shedding of all these was like the release of an albatross from around Clara's neck. Each dress, each carefully mended piece of inexpensive underwear, was a deeper burial of Solda, a securer lock to hold her in her grave during the dark, the fitful nights.

But there were the things which Clara could not leave, and still remain in character, the things with which no woman would ever part, no matter what her change in financial circumstances, or her lot in life.

These were the few small souvenirs of sentiment which were of Solda's childhood and, of all her young hard years in Minnesota, her sole mementos of sparse happiness, and of far sparser love.

A miniature china dog—a needlework impossible sailboat upon a flattened sea, with beneath its miraculous floatability a quotation from the book of Psalms: *He maketh the storm a calm, so that the waves thereof are still*—a child's saucer and cup, pretty with hand painted flowers—a sweet-grass sewing basket that had been her mother's—such was the modest list.

They were now disposed about the living room that had been Mr. Watertown's before his passage (via the attic) West. They were beginning to prey upon her mind, ever strengthening their hold in the indefinably sinister atmosphere of the neighborless house, and Clara would have given anything to destroy them, crush them to shapelessness, and hide them beneath the earth as Solda was hidden.

She dared not. The liaison between Mrs. Porter and Mrs. Lovestone was too complete. She knew that, on her days off, Mrs. Porter headed straight as a carrier pigeon, and told Mrs. Lovestone the least details of life in the house in the pines, just as Mrs. Porter would recount the most tedious details concerning Mrs. Lovestone on her return.

The living room itself, by all rules, should have been a cheerful one, for the furnishings were good and attractive with chintz, but its windows viewed, across a moderate carpeting of lawn, the acid green of somber pines, close packed, and corridored, beneath their lowest boughs, with avenues lost to the sun.

So absolute was the stillness that Clara was able to hear Joe's car approaching from a distance on his return from a shopping expedition in groceries for Mrs. Porter. She ran out on the driveway and flagged Joe to the front, before he could take the branch drive to the kitchen. It was wonderful how her nerves quieted just by looking at him, how the tight knots seemed to loosen.

Joe stopped the car and just sat looking at her and, for a perceptible moment, Clara just stood and looked at him. Nobody ever needs to talk, Clara thought. Not at certain times.

"Would you mind going to town again, Joe?"

"Certainly, Miss Carmandine."

"Get a couple of books and some magazines, will you? I'm down to the advertisements."

"Which books, Miss Carmandine?"

"Nothing heavy, Joe."

"All right."

Clara sat on the porch steps and rested her back against a fluted column. She'd have to be careful about Joe. You could get tangled up. You could get so tangled, so deep that you might even do something foolish. It was getting harder all the time when around Joe to remember she was Solda, that her super-fiancé Robert Johnson champed for a return from Peru, that the Porter-Lovestone liaison never flagged, and that Mrs. Lovestone mulled.

She wanted love, young love, not the attentive desiccations which had been Harold's, and which she had endured, most carefully endured, only because always the assurance was with her that some day she could cash in and blow. She wanted a love such as Joe's would be.

Often she wondered just how Joe felt about her. She couldn't tell. He was almost tiresomely respectful, and seemed on the defensive against the most innocuous, even, of conversational intimacies.

She shut her eyes against the stark and melancholy view while the sun dipped down, and after a while Joe was back, a lot of magazines in his arm, and handing her two books.

"Will these do, Miss Carmandine?"

Clara looked at titles: *Let Lie the Dead*, and *Good to the Last Mile*. She kept looking down on sleek, macabre jackets, and with all her will power prevented her fingers from clenching.

"The clerk in the store said they were escapist literature. I didn't know what he meant but he explained it to me. In an English accent. He said that the Last-Mile one was a riot. It's even got ghosts."

Clara, unseeingly, lingered along a blurb, then she did look up, straight into his strong and sunny smile. "They couldn't be better. Thank you, Joe."

CHAPTER 23

Sergeant Morris took his week's vacation in New York, and his wife, Freda, went with him. She had arranged with her sister Estelle to stay in the house with the children, to see that they got off in time for school, that Gracey be prevented from monkeying with the oven regulator of the gas stove (the child was a prima donna cook) and that Junior refrain from experimenting with his chemistry set until Papa was back, in case of pieces.

The Morrises stayed at a very good mid-town hotel and had a lovely time. They would meet around the cocktail hour and then either dress or not, according to what they had planned to do. They saw a few hit plays and revues and invariably ended the evening at a night club, drinking sensibly and dancing a great deal, a job which both of them thoroughly enjoyed, and did very well.

During the daytime Freda shopped.

Not Morris.

He spent the first forenoon at the Arts Club for women in the West Fifties where Davis had told him Clara had lived during her period in New York.

Sitting in her office, Miss Lamschalk, the manageress, was most helpful. She was a tall woman with a figure, gray, carefully coifed hair just off the bob, and with handsome features which just escaped the vulpine. Her voice, especially when talking with men, and especially so with men who looked like Morris, was artistically cultured.

"A Miss Clara Malden, Sergeant Morris? Just a *little* more than two years ago? The drama—one has so many of our dear girls who simply come and go—oh, you have a photograph of her?"

Miss Lamschalk permitted her brows a modest pucker, while she studied the picture of Clara, first taking in the smart, expensive costume and the circlet of jewels—yes, they looked very genuine—around her throat, then landing on Clara's face.

"Oh but of course, Sergeant Morris, I remember Miss Malden perfectly now. She was with us for somewhat over half a year. How is she?" (What Miss Lamschalk really wanted to ask was: What has she done?) "I mean, when one is questioned about someone by the police—?"

"She is—missing, Miss Lamschalk. I'm trying to back-trail her life, her associations from Blush Falls."

"Missing? How perfectly dreadful. So many people seem to be nowadays, don't they? I don't know what I can do to help you—beyond her application blank—I mean we were never intimate in a sense of confidences. One has so little time to be personal—"

"Could you look the blank up, please?"

Miss Lamschalk did, with a choice precision and flurry of pale, tapering fingers, which had once been favorably compared to ones in a sketch by Cellini.

"I'm afraid there is nothing but the barest facts, Sergeant Morris. Her home is listed as Richmond, Staten Island—age nineteen—parents both dead. She did tell me about that—a perfectly frightful automobile crash, which killed her dear mother. Her father, in his grief, passed on by jumping overboard from the Staten Island ferry boat. So Miss Malden decided to take up a career in the theater, and sold her little home in Richmond, and came to us."

"Who did she sell it to, Miss Lamschalk?"

"Wickers? Wilkers—yes, I believe she said it was to a family by the name of Wilkers."

"Had she any close friends among the girls here?"

"Yes, now that you speak about it, she did. Lola Marique—ballet, and Vivienne Ardmore—drama."

"Are they by any chance still living here?"

"Yes—oh of course, one understands—you want to meet them, to continue with your back trail."

"I would appreciate it very much."

It was arranged, and on separate occasions Morris lunched with each of the two young ladies. Miss Lola Marique (ballet) turned out to be a striking and vivacious blonde from the Corn Belt, while Miss Ardmore was an intense young creature, imbued with a fervid determination to knock Catherine Cornell straight off the boards.

Both of these artistes ate heavily, and Morris had selected for the luncheons the little French place on east Fifty-fourth Street where the fate-inspired meeting between Davis and Clara had occurred. The food and wine were good, and you could sit talking for hours without being glared out on your ear.

Unfortunately for Morris's purposes the talk had bulked overwhelmingly to monologues on Miss Marique's aptitude for ballet—even as a tot she had twirled around her home parlor, her neighbors' parlors, pas-seuled in the high school auditorium, all with immense reclame and vociferous admiration on the part of her beholders—and on Miss

Ardmore's past, present, and future plans for a brilliant attack on the stage—Portia, mind you, at the, age of four—that mercy speech, the "It droppeth" one—anyhow, she recited it for Morris.

What he gleaned from them about Clara was little. So little, in fact, that he decided Clara must have been a very good listener. Yes she had friends, very nice men, some young, some old, and did go out on dates, but she was careful. Very careful. Both Miss Marique and Miss Ardmore felt that Clara had been waiting for the main chance—if Sergeant Morris got what they meant, which Morris did. A few other unenlightening and unimportant odds and ends.

The manager and staff of the little French restaurant were equally unhelpful. One waiter, on seeing Clara's picture, vaguely recalled her having dined there several times. Always alone—no, on the last occasion a man had joined her. She hadn't been in again.

Meager stuff.

Greenwich Village, which the two artistes had mentioned as having been the locale of several of Clara's dated excursions, provided a quite interesting afternoon, but only insofar as its joints and general atmosphere were concerned. Nobody remembered Clara. She had, Morris decided, the damnedest ability either for circumspection, or for effacing herself.

A couple of other afternoons were spent in short visits to schools for dramatic art, and in completely useless delvings around the theatrical section of Broadway.

Staten Island brought Morris's touring to a close. The Wilkers family of Richmond were easy to locate. They were easy to locate, because they were one of the oldest families of the place, and had lived in their pleasant white homestead, which Clara was presumed to have sold them a few years ago, for more than three generations.

Mrs. Wilkers remembered Clara, when Morris showed her the picture, and, after getting over being outraged at Clara's lie about the sale, said that "that" Miss Malden had occupied a shore cottage for a summer about three years ago.

No, there was nothing *definite* that Mrs. Wilkers (unhappily) was able to say. The cottage was somewhat isolated—Mrs. Wilkers had called, just to be neighborly. She had found Miss Malden, well, self-centered and cold. A theatrical career or something—seclusion—just the same, cars had arrived over weekends—men, but (grudgingly) women with them too—no, there was nothing you could say, but you could *think*.

The agent Miss Malden had leased the cottage from? Ah, that was a tragedy! It was understood he drank. One night he fell asleep on a couch in his office—a cigarette, they thought—yes, burned up, himself, everything, all his records.

Well, Morris decided, it was like San Francisco. Behind the record-consuming flames, the wall was blank. Even though, in Clara's case, they could easily, and probably had been lies. He regretted it, though, for lies were often at times half-truths.

Freda, over cocktails, would always ask him what he had done (Morris never had to bother wasting his breath, asking her what she had done) and his list was catholic. It ranged from Radio City through ball games to—he crossed his heart, and managed a perfectly deadpan face—an edifying promenade with peanuts around the Bronx Zoo.

"This has done you a world of good, Walter," Freda said while they were packing for the return to Blush Falls. "It's been what you've been needing all year—a complete change."

CHAPTER 24

Harold and Edna were married in late October.

Under normal circumstances the wedding, no matter how quiet, would have been in shocking taste, so shortly after Clara's death. But the circumstances were not normal. All of Harold's and Edna's friends were strong for it, almost to the point of insistence.

Nor was it a union of passion, but rather one of lifelong friends who held an agreeable complacency of mutual social position, of age, of interests, and of tastes. There is no doubt but that a touch of the mother-complex entered subconsciously into it for Harold, whereas her deep affection, and her motive to alleviate his loneliness, offered the strongest motivation for Edna.

It was a marriage of absolute happiness, respect, and understanding. Gladly, and without a second thought, Harold would have laid down his life for Edna, exactly as he would have done so for his mother. His unspoken pledge was to shelter and protect her from all harm or freaks of circumstance, from any hurt throughout their lives.

Its repercussions throughout the town were varied. Among those who knew of, but did not know, Harold and Edna it was about a fifty-fifty split. Perfectly all right, and anyhow it was their own business, their own lives. Perfectly scandalous, the gossip went, and I've heard—of course I can't vouch for this—but you know Alice Dinkrest, don't you? Well—and then where there's smoke, you know, there's always fire—she lost all her money and needed his—he lost all his money and needed hers, that young wife of his who died had simply *eaten* it up—funny about her dying in that way—that accidental way—then his rushing into marrying a fortune—

That sort of stuff.

Clara read of the wedding in the *Gazette*, and the story was not without its newsworthy pinch of malice, carefully non-libelous, in its oblique lifting of the first Mrs. Harold Davis's rather recent tragic death.

While a fierce exultation turned her blood to heady wine, the Enoch Arden motif sprang clear before Clara with double-barreled force. Flicked from her memory were the sentient bits:

...the lazy gossip of the port,
And one, in whom all evil fancies clung
Like serpent eggs together, laughingly
Would hint at worse in either...

But strongest of them all:

So these were wed, and merrily rang the bells,
Merrily rang the bells, and they were wed.

Yes, Harold and Edna were wed, and Clara told herself, while this exultant feeling seemed to bathe her whole body with an electric glow, that the hour, soon now, would come for her to strike. Not too soon, but just long enough for Harold and Edna to feel the full and everlasting bonds of man and wife.

Mrs. Lovestone read the story while breakfasting nutritiously in her kitchen nook. Her well-bred swallows of coffee were alternated with well-bred gasps, until, unable to control her feelings any longer, she settled herself before the telephone and called the old Watertown place.

"Miss Carmandine?"

"Yes? Oh good morning, Mrs. Lovestone."

"I simply had to call you up. You've read the *Gazette*, of course?"

"Yes, Joe drives in quite early and brings it out."

"Well! Has anything ever struck you as more heartless? So utterly *un-comme il faut?*"

"I'm afraid I don't just—"

"The wedding—that Davis man—not having the common decency to wait for at least the conventional full year."

"But after all, Mrs. Lovestone—I mean, why should we—why should it affect us?"

"Because, Miss Carmandine, I cannot help but keep on identifying that poor drowned woman with you. As I still always say, the living *image*, and this shameless marriage when she's scarcely cold—my dear, it makes me boil."

"Surely, Mrs. Lovestone, isn't that awfully farfetched?"

"I know it, and I'll realize just how silly it is after a while, but mark my words—no good will come to him of it. It's a deliberate flaunt at Fate!"

Clara, with the exultation still filling her, could not resist saying: "Perhaps in that you're right."

"I know I am. Whenever *anybody* oversteps the bounds of social propriety, they trip." Having got this off her chest Mrs. Lovestone proceeded to further fields. "Now do tell me, Miss Carmandine, what you've heard from Mr. Johnson? Surely you must have had a letter by now?"

"By—now?"

"Yes, dear Mrs. Porter—she takes *such* an interest in you—told me none had come as yet when she dropped in to see me last week. We both hoped nothing could have, well, happened to him—what with the Andes." Clara grew a little chill, and thought fast.

"I'm just sure you'll understand, Mrs. Lovestone—we're both so alike in so many things, you and I—"

"Yes?"

"In our outlook on life, I mean—on the romantic side of life—"

"Oh Miss Carmandine, I really do believe we are."

"Well, it was a pact."

"A what?"

"A pact, Mrs. Lovestone, made between Robert and me. We both felt that letters, that any sort of communiqués, would only add to the poignancy of our being apart. We agreed only to write if one or the other of us was in some serious trouble or was badly ill, except that he was to send me a cable when he was starting for home."

"Miss Carmandine, I think that is one of the most beautiful, most exquisite feelings I've ever heard of in my life."

This drivel went on for a while longer, and then mutual expressions of good wishes were indulged in and we-must-see-each-other-soons, and they said good-by. Morris read the wedding story too.

His eyes were reflective with satisfaction, as he thought: So there could have been the "other woman" in the case.

CHAPTER 25

Foliage offered patterned massings of scarlet and bronze gold on the Indian summer's morning when Edna completed the last of her arrangements covering the closing of her house. A caretaker and his family were already at home in the service wing, and the garden, now pungent with asters, chrysanthemums and late roses, would be bedded for the lengthy winter after the first killing frost.

Edna had moved her own efficient staff to add to Harold's Effie and Agnes, and even now the ménage was beginning to run once more with the unobtrusive smoothness which had been obtained during Mrs. Arnold Davis's day.

Harold was waiting on the terrace, and together he and Edna walked through the garden, and along the bordered pathway with its rustic crossing over a brook, and through a copse of silver beech, which had always linked the two estates.

"Will you miss this, Edna?"

"How could I, Harold? Both places are one now."

"I know, but you get accustomed to familiar things, to a routine."

"It's you, dear, who will have to become accustomed to me."

"I think I always have been, Edna."

The house was warm and terribly comfortable, like a home again, when they entered its large hall, with its panel wallpaper of an early provincial design, and the slow upward curve of its graceful stairs.

Edna went up to her suite, which had been Mrs. Davis's and later Clara's, and saw that her maid, Elizabeth, was putting the last few things, which had been sent over during the morning, in their proper places. Harold, utterly at peace, relaxed in his favorite chair in the library before the pleasant antics of a birch log fire and read.

They lunched on a good warm vegetable soup, filet of sole, a salad, and strawberry tarts, prepared by Agnes. There had been a little contretemps about the cooking business which had taken all of Edna's efficient tact to resolve, for her own cook, Genevieve, was now on the staff too.

It turned out quite simply, really. Agnes was to boss and Genevieve assist, then Genevieve was to boss and Agnes to assist, on alternate days. When either would have her day off the other would reign supreme. It was really an excellent system, because the friendly rivalry between the two resulted in the turning out of consistently superlative meals, a fact which Harold vaguely noticed.

That evening they gave a small dinner followed by a quiet and agreeable reception for their more intimate friends. Edna had thought this wise. It would blend Harold more smoothly back into the normal sort of social life which once had been, and now would again be his.

There were several tables of bridge, a pleasant buffet (Genevieve—Agnes being pretty well done in by the dinner) with champagne, and two Chopin Etudes by Edna upon insistent request.

It was all very on the surface, but very sincere and very smooth. Not one word was mentioned touching on Clara. The past was tacitly imprisoned in silence.

Clara, for all of them, truly was dead.

CHAPTER 26

Mrs. Lovestone, to her utter astonishment, received a letter from Antonio Carmandine. Fortunately she liked puzzles, for Carmandine's handwriting was a honey, being spattered with strangely made and involved letter forms, some totally weird, and highly ornamented capitals, and a general disorderly mugginess which would have sent a trained graphologist for the nearest straitjacket, and into loud warnings concerning delusions of grandeur.

The gist of this scrabble was an imperative desire on Carmandine's part for broader enlightenment about certain points Mrs. Lovestone had so enigmatically touched on in her last letter to him in Minnesota.

Just what "fortune," what "luck" had she meant? For two months the puzzling over it had been driving him crazy. He was writing to Mrs. Lovestone only under the deepest compulsion, because he knew it would be no use to write to Solda. She would never answer.

He, poor discarded creature, was nothing but her dear Papa whose toil-weary fingers were worked to the bone, whereas Solda was a conniving, heartless, unnatural, and serpent's-tooth-hand-biting wretch. He commanded Mrs. Lovestone to sit right down and send him a letter telling him exactly what was what.

Mrs. Lovestone did just that. She was completely outraged and shaken at this brutal attack on her esteemed and, yes, beloved Miss Carmandine.

Solda, she informed him, was now well out of his clutches—you beast. She was engaged to a man of staggering wealth, one practically bowed beneath the weight of his Peruvian gold mines. The marriage was to take place by the middle of next year at the latest, but it would probably be consummated much sooner if Mr. Johnson could finish up his analysis of nuggets and get back from South America.

But even right now (Mrs. Lovestone galloped on, the bit well clamped in her teeth) Solda was a woman of large and independent wealth, thanks to Mr. Johnson's kind bestowal upon her of a private bank account.

Furthermore, she was living by herself on a fine old estate, the Watertown place, handsomely situated in a private forest just outside of town—Mrs. Lovestone with difficulty prevented herself from stocking this regal preserve with pheasants and a herd of deer.

So that, my dear Mr. Carmandine, was what was what.

Exhausted but still sizzling, Mrs. Lovestone made herself a pot of tea. Several cups and a raspberry jelly sandwich somewhat calmed her, enough so, at any rate, to permit her to put on her hat and coat, and go straight out and mail the letter.

What a brute, what a *perfect* brute, the brute must be!

On her return Mrs. Lovestone took Carmandine's letter and putting it in a saucepan set fire to it, crumpling the ash and dumping it into the garbage container. It was only after this ritual of purification had been completed that she wondered whether or not she shouldn't have shown it to Miss Carmandine. This now being an obvious impossibility she then wondered whether she ought not to call Miss Carmandine up and at least tell her about it.

She decided not. Solda had forgotten her horrible father.

Let him remain forgot.

CHAPTER 27

Clara had Joe drive her into town, as she wanted to go to the public library. The day was brilliant enough, so that her sun glasses did not, in spite of the season, seem too extreme. She had remembered, as she always remembered everything, Harold's strong interest in first editions.

She sat beside Joe on the front seat, and as always when riding with him, his nearness befogged the clear and cold and hard determination which ruled her life: the smooth and perfect pathway with the greatest and most independent sort of personal financial security.

Even right now, when she was on the brink of setting the machinery in motion for cashing in on her first important haul, the closeness of Joe's profile, of his hands on the wheel, almost made her want to throw her fixed determination out of the window. It both irritated and frightened her that she should feel this way.

"I've never asked you, Joe. Are you married?"

"No, Miss Carmandine."

"Engaged?"

"Not me!"

That stopped that for a mile or two.

"What are your plans in life, Joe? You don't mind my asking, do you?"

"Not a bit. What do you mean by plans, Miss Carmandine?"

"Well, I mean surely you're not going to do this all your life, are you?"

"What's wrong with this?"

"Nothing, I suppose, but where does it get you?"

"Where did being a stenographer in the mills get you, Miss Carmandine?"

"A—what—oh of course I see what you mean." (The Porter-Lovestone liaison, naturally through Mrs. Porter, would have been sliced off to Joe.) "Well it wouldn't have gotten me very far. I had to break loose, sort of take the bit in my teeth."

"Just so. And now you're marrying a rich man. Well, I intend to marry a rich woman. And if you don't mind my saying it, I'd like her to be a good deal along your lines, Miss Carmandine."

"I don't mind it a bit, Joe."

"Here's the library, Miss Carmandine."

Clara went inside the pleasant gray stone building. She said to the young woman librarian: "I wonder whether you would have time to give me some information, please?"

"I'll be glad to, if I can. Won't you sit down?"

"Thank you. I'm certain this won't take a minute. What I would like to know is the name of one book, any book, which would be of more than special interest to a collector."

"Do you mean among known items, the numbers of which are already established as extant?"

"Couldn't an additional one be discovered?"

The librarian laughed pleasantly.

"Well, anything is possible, of course, but with some items it would create little short of a cataclysmic sensation."

Clara smiled pleasantly back.

"Do tell me one of those."

The librarian mentally ran through a list and picked out one of the most extreme.

"How would an example of the second edition of Hamlet do?"

"Couldn't it be one of the first?"

"I can assure you that the second is infinitely more valuable. It's the first to contain the true text. There are only three examples extant—at the Huntington, the Elizabethan Club, and the Folger collection in Washington."

"Could I write that down, please?"

"Of course."

The librarian shoved a scratch pad and a pencil across the desk and rechecked the details for Clara.

"Thank you," Clara said, getting up.

"Do you mind my asking whether this is for a hoax?"

"Yes, it is. Yes, I guess you could call it that."

Clara said to Joe on the drive home: "After lunch, Joe, will you drive Mrs. Porter into town? She's spending the afternoon with Mrs. Lovestone."

"Certainly, Miss Carmandine. I hope you didn't think me fresh when we were coming in."

"Fresh?"

"My bringing up that business about your once having worked in the mills. You know how Mrs. Porter likes to talk."

"But why on earth should I mind?"

"Well, lots of people like to forget their past and not have it mentioned. When they step up, I mean. And then that other thing—about my hoping I could settle for someone along lines like you. It just came out."

"But I didn't mind at all. In fact it's very flattering. Look, Joe, why don't you stay in town this afternoon also, then pick Mrs. Porter up around five? Why not go to a movie or something?"

"Thank you, Miss Carmandine, I'd like to."

Well, there it was. The house, except for herself, would be empty.

The first small opening gun had been fired.

CHAPTER 28

It was wonderful, Harold thought during luncheon, how settled he and Edna were, even after such a brief few weeks of marriage. Not that you could measure it in weeks, nor through any of the media of chronology, unless you wanted to go Einstein about it, which Harold didn't, and certainly wouldn't have understood if he had.

"I've just been thinking that time means nothing, Edna. I mean it's as if we had been together always. Of course I suppose our having known each other since childhood has a lot to do with it, but it hasn't everything to do with it. Not by a long shot, Edna."

"No, dear. Far from a long shot. As for me, time right now means a lot. I'm due in an hour for that curious terminology known as presiding at the charity bridge at the Women's Club. What the job amounts to, of course, is simply keeping the peace."

"Yes, I saw a notice about it in the *Gazette*. For some orphanage, isn't it?"

"No, dear, the County Humane Society. I shan't be back until practically dinner. Those things linger. And you know, they don't do much good really—the charity parties I mean, not the Society. By the time the expenses are paid there's awfully little left to give."

"I'll make out a check to accompany you."

"No, dear, you will not. The treasurer has already told me what you sent. It was quite large enough. I'll make out my own."

Edna kissed him lightly, fondly, and went upstairs to get her things, while Harold contentedly wandered into the library to indulge in the middle-aged luxury of an after-luncheon nap.

Effie woke him shortly after two.

"It's the telephone, Mister Harold."

"Oh, yes Effie? Who?"

"A Mrs. Wiggins."

"I don't believe I know any Mrs. Wiggins."

"She says it's about a book."

"Oh, then."

Harold stood up and went to the telephone in the coat room. He occasionally got hold of some very good items in this fashion, from strangers who had heard of his interest from friends of some friends of some friends. Much more frequently, however, he would arrange an interview or go off on some lengthy chase, only to come up against some worthless, ancient tome that had been unearthed in the caller's attic.

"Mrs. Wiggins? Harold Davis speaking."

"Oh good afternoon, Mr. Davis. I have heard of your collection and I believe I've an item that might be of, well, more than ordinary interest to you."

It was an odd voice, Harold thought, almost as though it were muffled. Age? Yes, probably some dear old lady who had finally decided to part with her grandfather's heaven-knows-what edition of a copy of Dickens. It always hurt Harold dreadfully to disappoint them and sometimes, if they were very old and very kind, he would buy the wretched thing anyway.

"I'm always interested, Mrs. Wiggins. What is it?"

"It's a very good example of the second edition of Hamlet."

Harold controlled what might have been a derisive snort of laughter very well. Dear old lady or not, this really was going too far.

"I'm sorry, Mrs. Wiggins, but I'm afraid that that is impossible. There are only three—"

"Yes, I know," Mrs. Wiggins's voice broke in, "at the Huntington, the Elizabethan Club, and the Folger collection in Washington. Only you see, Mr. Davis, I happen to have acquired a fourth."

"Impossible."

"Surely you must realize, Mr. Davis, that during the past recent years a good many unknown, or if you prefer it, impossible caches were unearthed in Germany." Impossible. Even in Germany's loot it was impossible. The word kept repeating itself in Harold's head—and still, one never knew. The oddest miracles could occur. Take that stunning example of one of the earliest presses of the fifteenth century which Pike found behind the mirror of a Saratoga trunk—

"I wonder whether you would permit me to call and look at it, Mrs. Wiggins?"

"I was about to suggest, Mr. Davis, that you do."

"When would it be convenient?"

"Are you familiar with the old Watertown estate?"

"Yes, I know where it is."

"Then won't you drive out? Why not right now?"

"Thank you, I shall."

Harold, by now almost in a high fever, groped blindly for a coat and hat, and hurried at just this side of a dog trot for the garage. He used the station wagon, and the crisp fall air cooled his brow.

Caches in Germany—loot—no dear old lady then, in spite of the voice. And now that he came to think of it, the Watertown estate. What was she doing out there? He knew the story, of course, about the suicide, and also the general grimness of the setting. Well, if it was loot, probably smuggled in at that, it was a perfect setting. A daring adventuress? Would it be wise—after all, the F.B.I.—but also, after all, if it *were* a second edition of Hamlet—

Harold's foot pressed the accelerator to the floor.

CHAPTER 29

Clara replaced the receiver, and returned for the fourth time through the lonely house (Mrs. Porter and Joe were already off to town) to her room. The triple mirror of her dressing table assured her that Solda was entirely gone. Her hair was arranged in the fashion with which Harold was familiar. It was almost as good a job as Edmonde himself could have done. Her makeup had regained its subtle artistry.

With the moment at hand for which, as it seemed to her, she had been so eternally waiting, Clara's nerves were in an astonishing state of control. Her pressure was a trifle high, and her pulse somewhat faster than normal, but neither of these variations reached surface.

She walked downstairs and took up a position in one of the living room windows from where she could watch the driveway as it emerged from its somber tunnel through the towering pines.

It was useless to conjecture any further on how Harold would react. For days and days this had been a tireless game with her, even though she was sensible enough to understand that no human reactions could ever, with positive precision, be forecast.

Twenty minutes passed before she went to the front door, and stood waiting to open it when the bell would ring. Outside on the driveway a car door slammed, and impatient footsteps sounded on the porch.

When she opened the door she let it swing wide, and left it that way, stepping back a little so that the full light of day would calcium the now haunted tragedy she had arranged in her eyes.

"Mrs. Wiggins? Mrs.—"

The blood, all of it, seemed to have left him. His breathing became slow and shallow. His hands were cold flesh, lifeless on his lifeless arms.

"Hello, Harold."

"Hello, Clara."

"You'd better come in and sit down."

"Thank you."

Clara shut the door, then led the way into the living room. She suggested to this automaton who followed her that he take the lounge.

"Brandy, Harold?"

"I think if you don't mind, yes, please."

It was ready on a taboret. Clara poured two glasses and gave him one.

"Water?"

"No, thank you."

Clara sat in a chair almost near enough to touch him.

"I thought it best not to say anything over the telephone, Harold. Because of the servants. Because of Edna. That's why I said I was a Mrs. Wiggins and pretended about the book. I thought the shock—I thought you might blurt out my name—"

His eyes never wavered. They held the flat and leaden look of incredulity. His breathing continued slow and shallow.

"I simply cannot believe it. You can't be Clara."

"I am."

"She's dead."

"You did believe it, Harold. You do!"

"I buried her."

She went about expertly piercing this rebound into stubborn disbelief, this wish compulsion that the truth could not be true. He sat there blank, and still under shock, as she incisively highlighted their intimacies which only she and he could know.

He heard her on the fringe of his intelligence, and he said during one of her pauses: "She was drowned."

Clara brought up her reserves. She loosed the slender chain from around her neck and showed him the locket with its clip of baby's hair, but she did not let it leave her hand.

> *This hair is his, she cut it off and gave it,*
> *And I have borne it with me all these years.*

His hair. It gathered back into better focus, more swiftly than anything else could have done, his scattered senses. His breathing became somewhat more normal. No ghost, no doubt now, no nothing else but Clara.

"Mother's."

"Yes, Harold."

"Clara—tell me, Clara."

Clara did.

Her story was a minor masterpiece of fabrication iced on the solidity of partial truth. She returned to that long-past, fatal Thursday afternoon. After leaving the hairdresser's and while aimlessly shopping around town she had had the remarkable experience of running into a strange woman who resembled her almost exactly. Both of them, struck by this, talked, and a casual acquaintanceship sprang up.

They had tea together. Then, at Clara's suggestion—both she and the woman being free—they decided to escape the heat by going out to the camp. The woman's name was Alice something-or-other. Clara, after her terrible experience, no longer remembered.

They swam for a while in the cool of the evening, then ate a light supper, and then went in for a final swim by moonlight. Suddenly the woman was seized with violent cramps. Clara made herculean efforts to save her, but the woman had great strength, and Clara was all but drowned too.

There was nothing that Clara remembered beyond the moment when both of them were sinking, she tight in the woman's clutch, the roar, the agonizing pounding in her ears, and an indeterminate recollection of her head striking a submerged rock.

Evidently the shock, the horror, the sheer terror of death (and, of course, the submerged rock) gave Clara amnesia. There was nothing whatever that Clara remembered until she recovered her true identity in this house several weeks ago. This typically amnesiac recovery occurred immediately after she had tripped on the stairs and sustained a bad head blow when she fell.

Well, after her initial bewilderment and attempts at orientation, fate, which had always pursued her, caused a copy of the *Gazette* containing Harold and Edna's wedding story to be the first paper she saw. It was lying flat on the living-room table—on that table. It was a two-days-old edition, and she had evidently kept it, in her amnesiac state, because of the resemblance of the woman's picture with herself. So for two days Harold and Edna had been married. Clara was appalled. The marriage was an accomplished fact.

The servants here in the house thought of her as a Miss Solda Carmandine, and she did not disabuse them of this belief as she had hoped and prayed to figure out what it was best to do—for Harold, for Edna, and for herself.

Clara, with her consciously haunted eyes, struck the opening bars of her coda.

"Truly, Harold, I think an important thing that we must weigh in all of this—it's that we no longer love each other."

"Yes."

It was true enough but he wasn't ready for that yet. Confusion had returned more heavily, making it most difficult for him to think. Where (he wanted to know, and asked her) had she lived? How had she obtained her other identity of this Solda Carmandine? And what had she lived on during her period of amnesia?

With beautiful simplicity Clara offered the incontrovertible fact that she did not know. No sufferer from that disease did know.

Ever.

CHAPTER 30

Clara knew so well.

Her eyes slid past Harold, and then were held for an unnerving second by the miniature china dog on the mantel shelf. It was no longer a souvenir of sentiment which had been Solda's. It was Solda. And during that second's hypnosis of fear, just as the details of a lengthy dream in sleep can be packed into a second's meager time, more details broke through the barriers against memory, and confronted her with that murderous night.

The silent camp house, herself alone there now—

The complete removal of her makeup—new face, clever with a not-too-obvious distortion of the painted lips, the brows, the eyes, a weight of mascara, no longer Clara's face but the face of a tart—

The shoving of Solda's clothes and accessories into an overnight bag which had been around the camp for years—

The tidying of the camp, the traces of their supper dumped far out among the dense evergreens—

The long, long walk along the river road until she was picked up by a returning celebrant and given a lift into town—

The walk to her house, the bankbook, the papers, and the locket—

The long, long walk away from her house, then the hailing of a cab, and being driven to Solda's apartment, assured that the driver would never connect her new face with any later picture which might appear, on the discovery of Solda's body, with the socially prominent Mrs. Harold Davis—

The assembling and packing of Solda's things in the deadly hush of early morning—

The taking from its hiding place behind a loose base board (where Solda in a burst of endless confidence had told her it lay hidden) of frugal Solda's savings, which had been sizable because her wants had been so few, and Solda's small inheritance from her mother, all this when added to her own banked nest egg—

The cumbersome journey down the stairs in the still quiet house, quiet but for the scraping bump of a suitcase against a banister—

The night in its early morning hour of three—

A further walk—
An all-night drug store and phoning for a cab—
The station—
"I'd like some more brandy, please, Clara," Harold said.
The spell broke.

CHAPTER 31

Clara poured two glasses from the decanter.

"I'll do whatever *you* say about all this, Harold."

Well, it was simple enough for her to say a thing like that. Just now, just as she said it, the full enormity of the problem hit Harold in its lucid and shameless clarity. Whether he believed Clara's story or not, and there was a faint subconscious question of doubt even then that he did so, he was shaken almost to the point of being sick, because his main consideration was for Edna.

She, his worshipped idol with that ephemeral overlay of the mother-image which was always on her, she must be sheltered at all costs—never harmed—never, no never pilloried by the avid public scandal which his bigamous marriage, no matter how unwitting it had been, would cause. Its lifelong shadow would lie forever over Edna, now piled upon the disastrous brevity with which it had been consummated on the very heels of his presumed first wife's very publicized hideous death.

What *could* be done?

Clara was ready for this. Her blackmail took the form of "suggestion" cleverly concealed.

She said again: "I'll do whatever you say, Harold. Divorce—annulment—but when you think of Edna—I mean almost everything would have to come out publicly—just about everything, Harold." Then she plunged her harpoon. "There is one thing that I could do. I've been thinking of it every day and night. I could just disappear again, as if I really had died. Like that poem—the one about Enoch Arden?" She pulled out the tremolo stop now. "I could make my way somehow, make something out of my life, but I know that you'd never permit me to suffer, Harold—financially."

In complete confusion, because of any number of miserable repercussions which could hit Edna, he automatically agreed that there would naturally be no question on the financial point.

Say, Clara suggested, if he were to give her a lump sum of maybe several hundred thousand dollars, maybe around three hundred thousand dollars?

Harold was not a fool, and his sense of money values was jounced at this amount, to a degree where his reasoning powers almost cleared completely. It struck him that this could have been Clara's purpose all along, in which case logic insisted she would not have tried to save, but would have had to murder the woman who was buried as Clara.

Faintly this showed on his face, and Clara caught the possibility of his realization that murder could have been done. The balance, and Clara, waited.

Harold looked at it logically now. Suppose he did call Clara's bluff? Edna would understand, their friends would—that is most of them would—but the public scandal would be terrific, and no matter how it turned out, for years the case would be recalled and, piecemeal, Edna would have to face it—divorce or annulment—trial for murder, for Clara's story never would be swallowed unquestioned by the law—the whole rotten mess, with its hideous bunch of potentialities, hit Harold and he simply would not do it.

Never, while there was *any* sort of an out, would he suffer Edna to be dragged into it.

It could have been an accidental death. This he considered with complete skepticism. Murder, should it have been murder—yes, even murder—it was over and done with. The dead woman could not be recalled. What purpose remained to be served beyond the theosophical contention that an act of justice should be done? Just one among the myriad which never were? It was sophistry, but he bluntly did not care.

There wasn't much more. Having made the decision, Harold's acquiescence was on its surface agreeable.

A pinpoint of fear settled in Clara at this pleasant surrender, at this tacit evasion of Harold's from any further reference to the woman who was dead, and lying buried in his family plot. It was almost as though an unspoken bond of conspiracy were now between them.

What *did* he believe? Blinded by his determination to shield Edna had he accepted Clara's version? Or did he guess the truth?

Harold became quietly businesslike.

"A lump sum of that size is a little impractical," he said. "It means that securities will have to be converted into cash. Would two payments be all right?"

Clara restrained the avaricious eagerness with which she agreed.

"Certainly, Harold."

"I can manage the first within several days from now. Shall we say on next Thursday?"

"Yes, Harold."

"And the second about two weeks later?"

Some of the avariciousness did creep through as she suggested that the payments had better be made here in the house. She would arrange that the place would be empty, but for herself and for him.

It was a trivial thing when stacked against the moment as a whole, but Harold found it difficult to take his leave. This woman (he thought of Clara that way now) who once had meant so much, and to whom he so evidently had meant nothing but a bank account to be kept on ice for an opportune looting, filled him with a surge of disgust. It was almost as though something leprous were brushing close to him and Edna.

And though he felt this way, his ingrained habit of the essential courtesies by men towards women made it congenitally impossible (as he wanted to do) simply to pick up his hat and coat and go.

Actually it need not have bothered him, because Clara said: "Good-by Harold. Until Thursday."

She led the way to the door, and opened it.

He said: "Until Thursday."

She closed the door.

CHAPTER 32

It was the unearthly hour when night gives way to day, while stars dim out, and the eastern sky reluctantly relinquishes its darkness.

Edna (Harold decided this while thoroughly wide-eyed and flat in bed with his hands clasped under his head, and the pillows in lumps from hours of tossing) is living in a state of sin.

He hurried to add, for such consolation as it might give him, that the state was one of technicality only, and of law. The consolation was small.

This gloomy thought, so in keeping with that predawn hour when resistance is clinically accepted to be at its lowest ebb, was followed by a much more sensible conjecture about Clara. From the few stories he had read in which blackmailers were involved they were never satisfied. With an invariable cliché they would bleed their victims to the last cent. Would this well-beaten path be followed by Clara, after he had handed over to her her outrageously hearty lump sum?

No.

A tepidly assuaging realization took form that he, if he were driven to the wall about it, held as effective a whip hand as she did, because of the very possible jeopardy to her neck. Suppose it all did come out—never, never would it, while Harold could prevent it, to the utmost moment when he could maintain his shelter around Edna—but just suppose it were to reach official attention, where was Clara? She was saddled with that unhappy woman out in the cemetery, and her flimsy story about amnesia.

What was it Sergeant Morris had said of amnesia? On that afternoon when Harold had reported Clara as missing? Yes—"It seems that amnesia is getting increasingly popular these days—sort of a who-am-I? wave." Harold took time out to decide that he liked Sergeant Morris. No definable reason at all. Just liked him.

And now what about that unhappy woman in the cemetery? (Clara having been disposed of.) Who was she? Clara's picture had been prominent in the *Gazette* on the day when the woman had been found in the river. The resemblance had been uncanny. Even though the identification had been established as Clara, the other woman's disappearance, her complete dropping out of her social circle, and family life, was still, after all of this length of time, (great heavens it was months!) unquestioned and unaccounted for.

But was that true?

Because of the genuine sensitiveness and the fineness of his character Harold was only too able to translate himself into the place of her friends and her family. While the eastern sky slowly flushed he found himself sincerely distressed, horrified really, at what the unknown woman's loved ones so surely must be suffering in their anguish at wondering what had become of her.

Had another woman been reported missing in the general period when he had reported Clara as having been?

Had there been any inquiries, because of the remarkable resemblance, subsequent to the publishing of Clara's picture in the *Gazette*?

Dare he ask Sergeant Morris whether there had been any reports of such a missing woman, without jeopardizing Edna by arousing Morris's suspicions? What excuse could he make to see Morris? The meeting would have to be most casually handled, and seemingly by chance.

The sun shot an eye of flame above the distant hills, and Harold went to sleep. He woke at eight, and going into the bathroom, took a look at his face in the mirror. He looked a wreck. The ravages of the sleepless night, and of worry, were traced all over.

He returned to the old Clara routine—drops in his reddened eyes, an ice cold shower (which he loathed), a brisk rub, a down-and-up shave, and brilliantine on his hair. He did not risk the aid-to-grooming around his middle.

He did his best to appear his recent sunny and contented self as he walked downstairs, and greeted Edna who was already in the dining room.

He kissed her and she said: "How smart you look this morning, dear. Not that you always don't, of course. Kidneys, this morning. Broiled."

The last thing in the world he wanted this morning was kidneys, or breakfast of any sort, beyond cups and cups of strong black coffee. But he managed to attack them with a reasonable degree of enthusiasm.

He said, in the middle of an especially unwanted one: "I want to run into New York and see Wilkins, Edna, about changing some securities. Would you care to come with me?"

"I'd love to, Harold. When?"

"I thought we might catch the morning plane. I could see Wilkins this afternoon, while you shopped or something. I'll phone the Plaza for reservations and we can take in a show, then take the plane back tomorrow morning."

"Darling, it sounds perfectly delightful."

CHAPTER 33

Clara's initial exultation over the clockwork precision and success of her scheme was beginning to wear thin. With its culmination so close at hand, her impatience swelled to get it over and done with, and then to go. Swiftly to plunge back into that covering sea from which Harold had taken her, and this time with a fortune in her hands.

Her restlessness to shed Blush Falls, and this tightrope act she was performing, was enormous. As a matter of fact it was beyond restlessness, for when she looked at her condition honestly, she admitted that she balanced on the brink of fear.

All through last night she had examined each facet of Harold's afternoon session and departure, while his complacence, and the complete ease with which she had apparently put the deal over, began more and more to strike Clara as having been too good to be true. Caste-bound, stodgy, household-godded though Harold was, there could still be something up.

What? Well any number of things. Her opinion of his strength of character was pretty slim. Would he be *able* to keep it to himself, or would he break down and tell Edna? And if so, what about Edna? There was strength there, all right. In spite of her silly tinkling about of Chopin. Yes, decidedly that was one of the things that might be up.

Clara's nerves were already whirring toward what was to become a metallic shrill to get out of it. Baldly, to escape. For good and all from Solda. Wasn't *that* really the crux of it, and not Harold? Small things were assuming a disproportionate magnitude, and dominant among them were Solda's trivial souvenirs of sentiment.

These—the china dog, which had certainly done a job on her yesterday afternoon, the sampler, and the sewing basket of sweet grass—were besetting her flair for ranking as one of life's prime superstitionists into the grip of obsession. She was coming to believe that, in a mystical fashion, they were almost mortally inimical to her.

And still she could not, dared not really, bring herself to destroy them.

Tuesday night was no better. Such fitful sleep as she managed to achieve was tortured with dreams, from one of which she woke up with a strangled scream. She took a couple of phenol-barbitals and left the bedside lamp turned on. She attempted to read but the words meant nothing to her.

The thing that frightened her most was that she was growing frightened of being alone. All her life she had been superbly self-sufficient. Even as a child she had been completely satisfied with being with herself, companioned by her mental images and devious plans.

The east lightened and she got up and dressed, restlessly walking about the room, and smoking interminable cigarettes. She stood by a window, which overlooked the garage, for a long time, and looked at the windows which were Joe's. Even thinking of him, and looking at his windows like that was, in her present state of nerves, no good.

She messed up but did not eat the excellent and revoltingly hearty breakfast of eggs, broiled ham, and popovers which Mrs. Porter had prepared, but did drink several cups of coffee. She felt that if there were one more *cluck-cluck* out of Mrs. Porter, she would have to scream.

Later in the day, during her restless roving, she overheard through the open pantry door Mrs. Porter's end-of-a-telephone conversation with Mrs. Lovestone.

"—probably right, Adelia, and it may be simply the result of not hearing from Mr. Johnson—what?

"Pact? Oh yes, that. But in my opinion, for what it's worth of course, I think she's frightened about something.

"Yes, dear, *frightened.*

"I don't *know*, but you know perfectly well, Adelia, that there's never been anything wrong about my intuition. Take this morning, why she was nervous as a cat and didn't eat a bite of breakfast—what?

"Broiled ham, eggs and popovers and you know the hand I've got with *them*. Feathers. Then roving the house all day, and when I suggested she have Joe take her for a nice drive, why I thought she'd take my head off—not that she *said* anything, of course, but it was the *way* she said it.

"No, not a single thing for lunch either. That tomato bisque of mine—you know about the pinch of nutmeg—lamb chops and broccoli with a hollandaise sauce and an upside-down pineapple pie. My dear, as I brought things on, she looked positively stricken. It's a very good thing that Joe has a big appetite. I *hate* things wasted.

"Well, cigarettes—just one cigarette after another cigarette.

"All right, Adelaide.

"Yes, dear. Good-by now."

Clara left the pantry and went back into the living room. She thought: I've got to snap out of this. I've got to watch my step.

She ate, even though it almost killed her, the entire dinner, and presented Mrs. Porter with her expected calm and friendly Solda-self.

"I was so worried about you, Miss Carmandine," Mrs. Porter said. "It's a relief to see you like this again, and to see you eat."

"Oh I've always had occasional nervous attacks, Mrs. Porter, ever since I was a child. Our doctor out in Minnesota used to say they were nervous indigestion. They never last long, and I'm over this one now."

"Well, I'm glad. I'll fix a tray with sandwiches for you, so you can have it before you go to bed. To make up for your lost meals."

Clara controlled herself admirably.

"That would be awfully kind, Mrs. Porter. Thank you."

That Wednesday night was worse, and yielded Clara with fracturing nerves to a lowering Thursday, darkened and wind-torn by a November gale which whipped grotesque gestures from the whining pines.

She got up and, faced with Mrs. Porter's tray of sandwiches still on a table where they had spent the night, took care of them by breaking them up into bits and flushing them away.

Clara all but had to command Joe and Mrs. Porter to take the day off and spend it in town. To clear the decks for Harold. The last thing in the world either of them wanted to do was to be gale-tattered by going abroad, no matter how strong the pull for Mrs. Porter was Cecilia Clare at the Bijou in "Threnody of Thorns" (the tragedy of a good woman's blasted love, plus child), with a subsequent coffee party at Mrs. Lovestone's, or Kelly pool for Joe.

They thought her insistence strange, and Clara knew it, but her nervous system was in such a condition that she did not care. Storm or no storm, they had to be got out of the house.

With the breakfast things cleared up, Mrs. Porter, looking more moribund than ever, shrouded herself in the roll of wool, which it pleased her to consider a coat, and joined Joe in the car.

Clara stood watching from the living room window and waiting for the car to start. It did not. She could vaguely see their two heads turned toward each other, talking. After a while Joe got out of the car and walked toward the house.

Clara opened the front door.

"Forget something, Joe?"

"Well no, Miss Carmandine. It's Mrs. Porter."

"Yes?"

"She's sort of worried about you. About you're maybe not feeling all right. She was thinking that she shouldn't leave you here alone."

"Joe, that's very sweet of her but it's perfect nonsense. I feel fine. Haven't you ever had those days when you just want to be absolutely by yourself?"

"Well no, Miss Carmandine. Frankly I haven't."

Clara's voice, in spite of itself, grew a little sharp. "Well I have. I just like to have complete privacy—so that I can dream."

"Oh," Joe said doubtfully, "I get it. South America?"

"That's right, Joe. South America."

"That'll make Mrs. Porter feel better. Sorry to have bothered you, Miss Carmandine."

"It was kind of you, and sweet of Mrs. Porter, Joe. Thank her for me."

Clara stood in the open doorway until Joe was back in the car, and until it was off.

They were gone at nerve-wrenching last and the desolated house was Clara's alone. Not really alone, because Clara waited in the living room with its view of the tunneled pines, and always unseen, but sensed on the periphery of her consciousness, circled Solda.

CHAPTER 34

The morning dragged with the viscosity of certain nightmares, and so did the first hours of the afternoon. Harold had not indicated any set time. *Would* he come? Would he have the money? Would Edna come? Would he and Edna come? Would his lawyer come? The questions were a rat race through Clara's head.

He came at three.

He looked cold, and stern, and almost sure of himself, just about as much so as he ever could.

"Let me have your things, Harold."

"No, thank you, Clara," he said with formal courtesy. "I'll keep my coat on, if you don't mind."

So they stood there in the hallway, and he took an oblong, block-like package, carefully wrapped in heavy manila paper, from a roomy raglan pocket, and handed it to her.

"Here it is, Clara."

"Thank you, Harold."

"It's in hundred-dollar bills. Anything larger is rather difficult either to change or to bank nowadays, without a report somehow reaching the department of taxation. I don't know just how they do those things, but they do."

"That was thoughtful of you. It wouldn't have occurred to me."

"The balance is to be arranged the same. It will be ready two weeks from today."

"Thank you, Harold."

"Would it inconvenience you if I were to come in the evening rather than the afternoon?"

Clara briefly considered the problem of Mrs. Porter and of Joe, the trouble she had had this morning in almost leveraging them out of the house—but how stupid, there could be no trouble on *that* day, when the total loot would be in her hands.

Harold noticed her hesitation. He said: "It's a musicale which Edna is giving at the house, and—"

"But it will be perfectly all right, Harold. How is Edna?"

He stiffened, and his lips thinned.

"She is very well, thank you."

The flush of her present success, the feel of the oblong package actually in her hand, threw Clara right up again on her usual crest.

"I'm glad, Harold. And I want you to know that I hope this sacrifice I'm making will bring both of you happiness, all through the years."

He felt like striking her, and it showed on his face, and Clara, seeing it, barely held herself from stepping back.

He said: "May I make it eleven o'clock? Will that be too late? I've an appointment at the club."

"Eleven will be fine, Harold."

Clara thought: That was stupid of me about Edna, but he's over it, and anyway it doesn't matter. He'll go now, and I can count the money. I can touch it with my fingers, feel it.

"There is something I would like to ask of you, Clara."

Instantly she was on guard.

"Yes?"

"I want my mother's locket."

She had not known what to expect—papers to be signed, releases, dangerously legal things which might later be turned against her. Relief almost caused her to laugh in his face. She did say: "Oh, that," freeing the chain from around her neck and giving it to him. "Here, Harold."

He took the locket from her with a fierce eagerness, closing his fingers warmly about it, then shoving his hand deep in the raglan's pocket.

"Thank you, Clara."

Neither of them this time made the least pretence of any grace at parting. Harold did deposit a grave bow while his normally harmless and indecisive lips retained their stiffness, then he left, and pulled the door shut against the querulous pressure of the wind.

Clara turned the key in the lock.

A deep breath slowly drained all nervousness and irritability from her, brought a respite to the gnawing of her mystical dreads, and with the oblong package clutched in her hands, she ran upstairs to her bedroom, the door of which she bolted.

Her sharp scarlet nails ripped the manila wrapping, and then she counted the money on the bed, arranging carefully neat thin piles, each totaling a thousand dollars. It was hers. It was all there. Crisp—mint new-clean.

Snow blended with the whirring wing beat of the wind. Then more snow, and more, until the pines were robbed of their acid greens, and sank phantomlike within lost hills.

And Clara counted the money all over again.

CHAPTER 35

The moment with Clara intensified in Harold, to the power of a rip tide, his vicarious torment at the personal torment, which the friends and loved ones of the unknown dead woman in the cemetery must be suffering.

Clara's face which (had there been added to it the casual cruelty of markings left on the overlong unburied dead) had brought back to him that other woman's face. Added to this, the cheerless coldness of the wind and snow on the long drive home, all of those things served to prod him.

He successfully made a decision: something would, must be done.

In bed that night, during one section of his wakefulness, Harold concluded there was only one thing for it: he would have to check on Morris's movements. Tail him, Harold believed the professional term was.

Skillfully keeping himself obscure he would observe where Morris ate and, say, whether Morris dropped in habitually at any certain tavern. With this information under his belt, the "chance meeting and casual chat" anent the current status of the Missing Persons Bureau's list would be in the bag.

He remembered a book downstairs in the library, by an extremely popular British author of the adventure school, which had involved a considerable amount of sleuthing. It had struck Harold as having been quite authoritative, and he decided that, as he was wide awake anyhow, he might just as well go down and get it. For a few professional tips.

He did.

In bed once more, he leafed through, pausing to digest the more pertinent passages. As the book had been published at the turn of the century, it leaned rather heavily on disguises. It was impossible to tell what Chisholm Mort would turn up as next. His consummate impersonations ranged from costermongers through earls to ruddy cheeked old ladies purveying apples.

With drooping eyes Harold was beginning to wonder what he himself should do along those lines, when a last wakeful grain of common sense snapped him out of it with the realization that if he were in disguise during his chance meeting with Morris, Morris wouldn't know who he was talking to.

The drooped eyes closed tight.

During breakfast the following morning he remarked casually to Edna that he was on the trail of a first edition and wouldn't be home for lunch. It was even possible that he might not be home for dinner.

"Why don't you ask Kitty and her sister and John over for dinner and bridge, Edna? I don't like to think of your spending the evening alone."

"But I've spent ever so many, dear."

"I know. But it's different now."

"All right, I will. I love you, Harold."

"Well, Edna, I love you."

CHAPTER 36

At various moments of the day, which took him outside of police headquarters, Morris became increasingly and astoundingly aware of Harold Davis.

On his first exit from the building about midmorning, to pick up a package of cigarettes at Kinney's, Morris had immediately spotted Davis across the street planted before the window of Luber's Music Shop, and indulging in some sort of paralytic motion, as though he were trying to see out of the back of his head.

Davis then had followed him, in a manner somewhat suggestive of a shy crab, to Kinney's and back to headquarters again.

This sort of thing kept up until late afternoon, until Morris was forced to believe against his best common sense that Davis, happy in the belief of wearing a cloak of complete invisibility, was for God's sake tailing him. Morris, still letting Harold enjoy himself, wondered why.

He liked Davis. Every thing that he had found out about him, during his fishing tours on off hours, Morris had considered pretty good and fine. Davis's present home setup and life were sound. His unpublicized charities were large and humanly sprinkled with a good many individual cases, which Davis handled personally, and with a warm almost-diffidence which abnegated any atmosphere of patronage. Yes, a right guy.

But now this.

Davis *couldn't* be tailing him. There was no sense to it, and certainly there wasn't anything else to it. What then? Could it—yes, it could be— Davis could be waiting for some opportune moment in some convenient spot, where Davis could straighten up from his impersonation of a crab, and breeze in with a "Well, well, think of meeting you here."

Lots of times it was done, only with about ten thousand percent more finesse. And still—why? Morris sincerely hoped that he didn't know the answer to this. That he was completely wrong. He liked Davis.

Towards five o'clock Morris allowed himself to be met by chance by Harold in Hogan's grill and bar. His surprise at running into Harold like this was a work of art. Over highballs, he continued to permit himself to be led.

It was a fluttery sounding-out which Harold went in for, and inept. Morris saw through the plate glass overture with the easiest clarity, while maintaining his stand of casual answers to the casual interest of a man who was politely interested in the labors of the Missing Persons Bureau.

So this was it, all right.

Harold in the intense absorption of his role with its, to him, pitiful and tragic purpose had had no lunch beyond a milkshake hastily downed at a drugstore close to headquarters. The window end of its soda counter had afforded a splendid, oblique view of the objective under Harold's observation.

As a result of this unaccustomed absence of a midday meal the second highball (this time on Morris) while not exactly going to his head, did loosen up the guards he had held on his tongue.

It had occurred to him in the night during his persistent thinking about different angles of the matter that Clara—supposing on the wildest chance that her story just might be true—could conceivably have adopted the identity of the woman who had been drowned.

He remembered Clara having said that she thought the woman's name had been Alice something-or-other, but she couldn't remember. But the point which appealed to Harold was that when Clara had come to, on tumbling downstairs and bumping her head, she had come to as a Miss Solda Carmandine.

Furthermore, the old Watertown place was obviously under rental to, and had been staffed by a Solda Carmandine and Clara was accepted by the staff. She and the drowned woman had been alike as-two peas—ergo, had not the drowned woman *been* Solda Carmandine?

His psychiatric familiarity with retrograde amnesia being on a par with his sleuthing, the conception had appealed to Harold as being logical and neat. Anyway, his tongue guards down, it seemed at the present moment to be worth a cast, one adroitly masked in subtle camouflage.

Morris restrained a sad flare of elation which was brought him by this significant nail just pulled by Davis from the coffin lid of the dead.

He finished his highball before saying: "No, Mr. Davis, I don't recall the name of Carmandine as appearing in any of our cases."

"Well, I must have read of it occurring in some other town."

"No doubt."

Harold made a show of looking at his wrist watch. "I'm afraid I shall have to run. Good-by, Sergeant Morris."

"Good-by, Mr. Davis."

Morris waited until Harold had gone, and then went back to his office. He looked in the telephone book. He looked in the city directory.

He called the man in charge of private files on the house phone.

"Jim, this is Walt. See if you've got anything on a woman by the name of Solda Carmandine, and call me back, will you, please?"

Jim, when he called back, had nothing, and Morris hadn't really expected that he would. She'd have been a worker, he decided, because you could suddenly drop out of a job, and rarely would anything be done about it. It would be taken for granted that you'd got another job somewhere else, and somebody else would just be hired to fill your place. Whereas if you dropped out of a family, or a circle of friends, something always was done about it. So she probably had worked here, and had come from out of town, and either had no folks, or else had had a row with them, and they no longer cared about her.

The idea was worth a shot, but it was too late to do anything about it tonight. The principle industry was the mills. They offered the biggest pay, and they drew girls from all over. Tomorrow he'd give them a ring.

He got in his car, and drove home where Freda announced that Junior had mixed up some fantastic concoction with his chemistry set—no, dear, he isn't hurt, but come in here and look at this rug. It's lace.

CHAPTER 37

The third mill telephoned to—the Frankton Mills—produced most gratifying results. Yes (a Miss Briscombe of the personnel department told Sergeant Morris) there had been in their employ a Miss Solda Carmandine. She had been secretary to their Mr. Allwhite and had, upon his transfer to Georgia, resigned.

Miss Briscombe remembered the matter very well, as she had handled it. Miss Carmandine had expressed her intention of taking a vacation of indeterminate length, and of indeterminate nature, and locale. This had struck Miss Briscombe as being, frankly, a bit flighty, but after all it was Miss Carmandine's own life, and she was the one who had to live it.

She was listed as living in the Lovestone Apartments on Ashcourt Street. When? Miss Briscombe named the date of the resignation in August—you remember, Sergeant Morris, that was Farmers Day.

Was, Miss Briscombe wanted to know with pardonable curiosity, anything—wrong?

No, Morris assured her, just a routine sort of an inquiry from a maternal aunt in Iowa, who hadn't heard from her niece in some time. Such trivia were but daily grist in the Missing Persons Bureau's mill.

Oh? Oh.

Morris looked up the street number address of the Lovestone Apartments in the telephone book, and jotted it down.

Fanners Day. He checked back. Yes, it was on Farmers Day when Mrs. Harold Davis had disappeared.

He continued with the morning's ordinary routine of his office. He added to his file of curiosa a frantic inquiry about a missing Letitia-Mae who turned out (when he could get the hysterical woman on the other end of the wire to calm down) to be a Persian cat—"I don't *care*, Sergeant, I tell you that to me she was a person, she was my family, Letitia-Mae was my *whole* family"—and on, and on, and on.

Toward noon he arranged to take the balance of the day off, and left his assistant in charge. He drove home. He told Freda that he was going on a special assignment, and changed into a grey tweed suit.

"What sort of an assignment, Walter?"

"I'm looking for a Letitia-Mae."

"What happened to her?"

"I don't know. She's a Persian cat."

"Oh really, Walter, there are times! Aren't you even going to have any lunch?"

"No, no lunch. She might be out."

"I think I'll get myself psychoanalyzed to find out why I really married you."

"Something awful in your childhood, dear. It always is, and you pay about five hundred bucks for the knowledge. Skip it."

He kissed her and left. He drove to Ashcourt Street, where Mrs. Lovestone received him, with the becoming dignity of an apartment house owner, in her living room.

Morris took a look at Mrs. Lovestone, and his pulse went a beat or two faster. Sure she was. She was the woman at the funeral who, in her "best" dress, and that horticultural hat, had viewed the body to the accompaniment of a tear or two dropped into a handkerchief with a border of Brussel's lace.

He was, he told her, a bachelor. His job was that of an accountant at the mills, and he was sick of living in that box which the hotel euphemistically called a room. You were never entirely in it.

Mrs. Lovestone was quite taken. So sturdy! So plein-air! So—yes, so agreeably charming.

Tm really very sorry, Mr. Morris," she said, and was, "but right now there isn't a single vacancy. Would you care to have me put you on my list?"

"I would appreciate it very much."

Mrs. Lovestone, at the desk, made a great show of elegance with paper and pen.

"And the name of your hotel, Mr. Morris?"

Morris mentioned a small hotel, the manager of which he knew, and who would arrange that he was always out, but that messages would be taken.

His eyes had not been laggard. Almost on entering the living room he had spotted a cutout in passe-partout of the *Gazettes* picture of Clara Davis from their special edition on the day when the body had been found.

Mrs. Lovestone had kept, and centered this, as a memento of what she had considered, and still considered, to be one of the extraordinary interludes in her usually humdrum life. It hung on the wall beside a picture of Albert and herself in a rolling chair on the boardwalk of Atlantic City, which in turn was flanked by a fading enlargement of a string of fish which Albert, during a fit of madness, had insisted upon their going up and catching in Maine.

"I feel," Morris said, "as though I had seen this picture somewhere before. Wasn't it in the paper or something, about something?"

Mrs. Lovestone leaped, with the presumed pleasure of an about-to-spawn salmon, into her favorite topic.

"Of course you did, Mr. Morris. It was in the *Gazette*, on the day they found her in the river. Surely you remember—Mrs. Harold Davis, the socialite?"

"Well—yes, I do remember something vaguely about it. Usually I stick pretty closely to the sporting page. Was she a relative of yours? I mean, you having her picture on your wall—"

"No, there was no relationship at all. My family were the Withermores of Alabama. But truly, Mr. Morris, there were the oddest set of *coincidences*."

"Between you and this Mrs. Davis?"

"No, it had nothing to do with me personally—I simply brushed the fringe—but between Mrs. Davis and a tenant, who is also a very dear friend of mine. A Miss Solda Carmandine."

"Really? I think that coincidences are fascinating. Don't you, Mrs. Lovestone? I mean like when you coincidentally run into a friend on a street corner whom you wanted to see."

"Oh but this was *much* more coincidental than that, Mr. Morris. Much! If you only had time—I mean you *are* due back at the mills soon, aren't you?"

"As it happens, I'm not. I've taken the afternoon off to go apartment hunting."

"Then—if you would care to sit down for a moment, Mr. Morris?"

Would he!

Mrs. Lovestone, once in full swing, spilled all. Rarely, if ever, had she had such an attentive, such a satisfactory listener. The minutes passed almost to the length of an hour and there was nothing, when the machine ran down, that Morris did not know, which Mrs. Lovestone knew, about Solda Carmandine.

"That point," he said, while at last she breathed, "about the sound at three o'clock in the morning—the automobile outside—the bump on the banisters. It was awfully clever of you to think of it as a suitcase."

"I said to myself at once, Mr. Morris—that is a suitcase bumping the banisters."

"So few people are so perceptive. I suppose Miss Carmandine's finger is all right by now? The one which was bandaged?"

"Oh yes, quite."

"Then she is able to send you notes, of course."

"No—no, Mr. Morris. I have myself dropped her an occasional little note or two, but she always replies by telephone."

"Mrs. Lovestone," Morris said, standing up, "I honestly can't begin to tell you how interesting this has been. But if I'm to do anything about an apartment this afternoon, I must tear myself away."

"Again I'm so sorry that I have none vacant, but I'll telephone at once, Mr. Morris, in case you haven't succeeded in locating by then."

There were mutual good-bys and Morris, feeling positively glutted, left.

He sorted, evaluated, and stored in his neat mind the bagful of lurid marbles which Mrs. Lovestone had poured so fulsomely into his hands. He attended to this while attending to a good broiled steak with draft ale at his favorite chop house.

Then, being further glutted still, he took a leisurely drive out and past the old Watertown place. He parked his car off the road in a clearing among desolate scrub, then walked back.

He made his way through the concealing pines to the edge of the lawn and found a spot where, without himself being observed, he could observe the house. Two hours of infinite patience went by, as did nothing else. Then a car turned in from the highway, and before it had gone very far along the drive the front door of the house opened, and a young woman came out. She talked for a moment with the very handsome driver of the car, and then went back inside the house, while the car continued on to the garage.

The driver, according to Mrs. Lovestone's soufflé about him, would be Joe.

The young woman would be Solda Carmandine.

The house, the grounds, with their brooding silence, were blank again. What a truly ideal spot, Morris thought, for a resident ghost.

He returned through the pines to his car and drove home.

"You're back earlier than I thought you'd be," Freda said. "One trusts you found Letitia-Mae?"

"Do you know, Freda—it's possible that I did."

His dear daughter Gracey leaped upon him shrieking.

"I made a cake!" she shrieked.

"Yes, dear," Freda agreed acidly, "you did. And your father will arrange to have the man put the oven regulator together again tomorrow."

CHAPTER 38

Clara held a tight enough rein on her nerves during the daylight hours, which were leading toward that Thursday of the final payment, to put through a carefully detailed preparation for swift flight from Blush Falls. She wanted no loose ends left, which might lead to the least confusion or speculation.

Her blanket excuse for this imminent departure was a radiogram, one fictitiously received at the house by her during a shopping tour of Joe's in town, and while Mrs. Porter was bemused in the deep sleep of an habitual afternoon nap.

Robert Johnson was concluding his affairs in Peru, and wanted his fiancée to meet him at the airport in New York City on a week from Friday. Such was the story Clara told Mrs. Porter, and Joe, Mrs. Lovestone, and the real estate agent Artemus Simms.

She settled with Simms for a cash payment of four months' rent for permission to break the lease. Mrs. Porter was informed that she would receive a bonus of an additional month's wages.

Mrs. Lovestone naturally necessitated a more formal note. Clara had Joe drive in and bring her out to a coffee session of more-than-usual elegance. As Mrs. Porter was to be present as a guest, Clara had insisted that everything but the coffee should be ordered, and called for by Joe, from the town's leading caterer.

The three sat in the living room with its glow of lamps, as the outer day faded to swift fall twilight, and sipped coffee while unostentatiously putting under their belts (Mrs. Lovestone's and Mrs. Porter's belts) a bewildering array of handsomely iced petit-fours and other small confections of the most delicious and expensive sort. It was indeed a red-letter, and bicarbonate-of-soda, day in Mrs. Lovestone's life.

At last it was over, with one polite petit-four left on the plate. There were kisses, and Clara assured Mrs. Lovestone she would be kept in touch with to the extent which Robert's interests would permit (they naturally kept him in a dragonfly state of constant dartings about the globe—India—Egypt—Saudi Arabia—who knew?) and once wed, she would accompany him.

Mrs. Lovestone, in a global daze, draped herself in the silver fox scarf and left. Mrs. Porter returned to the kitchen.

Those things being taken care of, there remained Joe. It was a decision which Clara found very hard to make: not taking him with her. Nothing had ever been said, beyond that brief raising of the curtain during the ride to the library, certainly nothing had been done, and Clara's coldly calculating common sense dismissed the remotest possibility that there ever would be.

She loved Joe. She knew that now. In all the amoral and iceberg fastnesses which composed her whole being there was that single warm, true flame. It had never happened to her before, and Clara considered it likely that it never would again, certainly not along the golden path which now lay so positively before her.

Even she herself appreciated that this weakness was out of character but that didn't alter the fact of its existence. It was stupid, it was absurd, but Joe had come to be the one important thing which, with absolute honesty, she had wanted in her brief life. His own stated calculated hardness of philosophy meant nothing to her; if anything she found it admirable as it paralleled so closely her own.

And she couldn't have him. Not even for a while. Blush Falls, and all that was in it, must be a chapter dead, for deadest of all must be dead Solda.

All these various arrangements had necessitated several trips to town. It seemed passingly odd to Clara, and of complete unimportance, that she had happened to notice the same stranger twice. Or had it been three times?

He was a man in his late twenties, well set up, with an intelligent and pleasantly plain face. Clara had noticed him no further than it was her custom to notice all men, and he was always on his way in the pursuit of his own affairs, but it did seem sort of funny how their paths would re-cross.

Well, in such varied fashion Clara passed her days. The black hours of the bead-strung nights were for her, however, something else again. Harold and Solda filled them all, and towards the close it was mostly Harold.

Each dark successive hour in the silent house had augmented, with its drop-by-drop of water, her conceit that Harold could be out to get her, and in time the drops formed a sizable pool of primitive fear. She could not rationalize herself out of it, any more than she could do so with her feeling for Joe.

The real trouble was that she had rationalized herself into it. If she could have committed a murder why couldn't Harold commit one too?

Of her. It would certainly make everything dandy for Harold if she were dead. No more worries then for him about himself and Edna. No future with a potential sword of Damocles above his head.

Clara's own strong aptitude for scheming convinced her of the deed's simplicity. She had established her identity so very soundly as Solda, and if she were to be killed, no conceivable connection would ever come up between a Harold Davis and a Solda Carmandine.

She kept putting herself in Harold's place. An accident on the night of the final payment would be so easily arranged in the private recesses of the house, deplete of witnesses as it would be with, Joe and Mrs. Porter having been paid off and having gone.

A fall downstairs and a broken neck. That was exactly how simple Harold could make it.

Unquestionably Clara was working toward a general crisis of nerves. There were even moments when she pondered the advisability of being satisfied with half, just to take the money already in hand and skip. But each time this powerful urge would beset her, her greed would damp it out.

The hag-ridden nights kept right on ticking off, and soon there were left very few.

CHAPTER 39

In the office of the Imperial Cab Company Morris said to Elsie: "This goes back to Farmers Day. There's little if any cruising done during the early morning hours, is there?"

"None, Walt. A couple of the cabs hang around the railroad station, that's all."

"Then if a call came in, say shortly after three in the morning, would you still have a record of it?"

"Certainly. Just wait a minute and I'll look it up." Elsie went through a ledger and said: "There was one at three-ten from that all-night drug store over on Ashcourt Street. Pete Kuffman took it."

"What's his address?"

Elsie gave it to him, and Morris thanked her. That was one of the many nice things about Elsie. She was as normally curious as any other woman but she kept her curiosity to herself.

Morris went to Kuffman's boarding house and woke him up. He sat on a chair beside the bed.

"Sorry to wake you like this."

"That's all right, I'd have been up soon anyhow. What do you want?"

"You got a call at three in the morning of the night of Farmers Day. It came from that all-night drug store on Ashcourt. Do you remember it?"

"Yes. I remember everything about Farmers Day. I'll settle for there never being another. This call was from a woman with a couple of bags and a portable radio. She wanted to go to the station."

"What did she look like?"

Kuffman gave a lurid description. "But," he said, "she didn't act like one."

"Did she strike you as being nervous or upset about anything?"

"No. Why? What's up?"

"I'm just trying to check one of the missing persons list. What was her voice like?"

"It was just a voice."

"What I mean is, did it go with her getup?"

"Well, she didn't say much, but now that you mention it, it didn't. It was sort of cultivated—you know, real lady stuff, or else a good imitation of it."

"Was she in a hurry to catch any special train, or anything?"

"No, she took her time. Just sat in back, and smoked. Paid me at the station and I got a boy to take her bags in.

"What time did you get to the station about?"

"About twenty of four."

"Do you know the trains that would be coming along?"

"Sure. I take my turn working them. At that time there'd be nothing but the four twenty-five—that's the milk train going south. It stops at every cow."

"Thanks."

"Okay. Anytime."

Morris drove back to his office, and continued with the daily routine. He succeeded in nipping the career of a fourteen-year-old frustrated mariner at the bus terminal, and returned him to his less sea-minded parents. His men located an overnight-absent husband blissfully celestialized in Murphy's Taproom, and returned him, with sympathetic reluctance, into the clutches of his Neolithic wife.

And the usual array.

Toward six he closed up shop and drove home. He enjoyed an excellent, and happy family dinner of a brisket of beef, a lemon meringue pie, a wife, and two children, for they were as much a part of every meal as the food itself. The minor cataclysms of events at school were thoroughly, and at times piercingly, gone into and the imminent Halloween party lasted through the pie.

"Gracey unearthed that ghastly copy that you have of Dante's Inferno, dear," Freda said. "The one with the Doré illustrations. She wants to go to the party as one of the semi-damned souls on page two hundred and twelve."

"It's much more original than a witch," Gracey said.

"Granted. And swallow that pie before you talk."

"Well why can't she, Freda?"

"Because, Walter, the costume would consist of an agonized expression, a coiffeur of snakes, and a few wreaths of smoke."

"Save you all sorts of bother."

"Oh really, Walter! She will go as a witch just like the rest of them. And Junior shall go as an imp. And I don't want another word out of either of you about it." There wasn't.

"Where's that alarm clock that used to be kicking around here, Freda?" Morris asked.

"It's on the shelf over the stove in the kitchen. Why, Walter?"

"I want to get up at three o'clock."

Freda thought this over.

"More cats?"

"No, the same one."

After the dishes were done Freda and Morris drove to the Bijou where he thoroughly enjoyed a murder mystery.

They went home and to bed, and at three o'clock the alarm clock rang, and Morris got up and dressed. "Good cat-hunting, dear," Freda said drowsily.

"I thank you, Freda. And may all your dreams be of Gracey and the oven."

Morris got out his car, and went to the station. He checked it in at a parking lot. The waiting room was empty, as he had expected it to be. He had no difficulty in having the ticket agent recall the woman who had bought a ticket toward four in the morning on the night of Fanners Day.

"Sure I remember where it was to," the agent said. "It struck me as nuts. Can you imagine getting up at that time in the morning to go twenty-five miles? It was to Brickerville, the next stop south."

"Give me one, will you, please?"

"You got a car?"

"Yes."

"Well you can drive there, man, before the train gets in here even."

"Maybe she paid for another one on the train. For some stop further along the line."

"I get it. Well, here you are."

"Thanks."

Morris had coffee and doughnuts in a diner.

The train came, and the conductor remembered the woman. She was the only passenger who had boarded it at Blush Falls. She had got off at Brickerville.

Morris knew Brickerville reasonably well, mostly just from driving through it on pleasant Sundays, with Freda and the children, on their way to a favorite picnic spot up in the hills. It was smaller than Blush Falls, but not close enough to being a village to be nosey. It had a couple of hotels, and Morris tried the one closest to the station.

It was it, all right. The night clerk remembered the woman very well. A Miss Solda Carmandine. He remembered her especially because when she checked in she looked like a you-know-what—brother, what a makeup!—whereas the next time he saw her, and for the balance of her stay, she looked like a nice, wholesome—well, you might almost say like somebody's sister.

"How long was she here with you?"

"For just a week. She got in just about this time on Friday morning, and left the following Thursday afternoon."

"Do you carry the *Blush Falls Gazette?*"

"Well, not here in the hotel. Wilkin's stationery store over on Fitch Street carries it. Mostly we read either the New York papers or our own weekly, the *New Englander.*"

"Would you know whether Miss Carmandine got any messages, or any mail while she was here?"

"No, she didn't. We were sort of wondering about that. She just stayed mostly in her room, and even fixed it to have her meals served there. She'd only go out about once a day, to get the papers or some magazines. We figured she was just taking a good, quiet rest. Too bad she's turned up on your missing list, Sergeant."

"Well, we'll locate her."

Morris caught the six o'clock back to Blush Falls.

He was a very bemused, and a very puzzled man.

CHAPTER 40

Edna supervised the bedding-down of Harold's garden, and of her own after a hard, killing frost had blackened the dahlias and left the asters limp. Only her cushion chrysanthemums had come through, and they, with their tints of bronze and rose and crimson, would still be good for several weeks.

Each late fall season when Edna attended to this she would feel a nostalgic sadness for the color and fragrance of the flowers which were gone, but then she would consider that a fresh young generation from their roots would take their places in the spring.

She cut some of the new Marjorie Mills mums for the house while wondering (the thoughts of spring had put it in her head) whether a trip of some nature wasn't indicated for Harold. During the past two weeks he hadn't seemed quite himself.

It had not struck Edna that the trouble was anything physical, but rather as though something were worrying him. Perhaps if they were both to run down to Pinehurst for a while? Virginia Springs? Change was always good. Having guests in rather frequently was too.

She spoke to Harold during dinner about Pinehurst, and he liked the idea very much. They could drive down, just the two of them—say on all the little out-of-the-way roads—and make sort of a jaunt of it.

This happily settled, Edna said: "I think I'll ask the Athertons to stay over after the musicale tomorrow for dinner. We'll have a good game of bridge."

The knuckles of Harold's sensitive fingers were suddenly tense and white on the silver. Bridge games could, in fact inevitably did, last well over eleven o'clock.

"Tomorrow is Thursday night, Edna."

She pretended not to see his tension, the slow drift of color from his face.

"Yes, dear. It's the afternoon of the musicale. Would you rather I didn't ask them?"

"It's just that I've been roped in for a game at the club. Couldn't we have them the following night?"

"Certainly. I'll ask Minnie whether they can come Friday."

After dinner they sat before the fire in the living room and talked, and Edna went on with some petit point for a chair seat, and Harold fitfully read. It was an atmosphere of the most deep, quiet intimacy and Edna brought up a subject that had been increasingly coming closer to her heart.

She wondered, and asked Harold, whether he felt as she did. They both had long, and sheltered, and companionable lives before them, but when they died it would be more than just the death of themselves. Their home, their—she found it very difficult to express—well *all* of themselves would die, even people's memories of them.

If there were children, even if there were adopted children, but anyhow someone whom they loved and who would love them when they were old and going, just to know that someone younger of their own were coming along, would stay—did Harold feel as she felt? She had wanted children, wanted them terribly.

A wind had sprung up, outside and was shaking one of the casements while a back-draught puffed an instant of smoke from the hearth.

"Yes I do, Edna," Harold said. "I think that at heart I always have."

Later, when Harold was in bed and had turned out the bedside lamp, he felt that the torment of his problem was complete. For added to their own, there could always be over the heads of their children, the threat of Clara. He was the kindliest, and most equable of men, but it was also true that never during his peaceful, even life had he been faced with any situation which could have aroused him and thrown him into fierce defense.

Never until now.

The money, that good lump sum, began to pale into insignificance before the slow and unaccustomed molten stream which began seeping into his veins. Clara. In a year, in two at most, the money would be gone. And with the years all his would be gone, because he knew the way she spent.

The strange and turgid stream in his veins was, in analogy, like cold fire because his mind seemed so cold and clear above its heat. The panorama of the coming years circled in review, and they became a hell, and he himself the lonely shield against that hell between his loved ones and Clara.

Unless Clara were to die.

She would never die.

But if Clara were to die.

Could he live with Edna, with children, could he live with himself, with murder on his hands?

Could he kill?

Harold's thoughts had become as frank as that. He was honest enough to indulge in no sophistries. Nor did he conceive any plans, for probably of all people on earth he least had the murderer s mind.

But the molten stream remained, and he carried it with him, at last, into sleep.

CHAPTER 41

Thursday morning broke broodingly, with the sun in retirement behind masked banks of storm-heavy clouds, and as the hours progressed, they advanced their grim battalions clear across the sky until no blue was left. There was no wind at earth level, and the pines could have been carved of dark marble against the darker hills.

Clara sustained a flicker of relief that the night was done: her last one at Blush Falls. It had been a corker, with the most fitful spells of sleep which was not sleep, but rather dreams, each one of which had been so sharply etched with the acid bite of fear.

She would not endure another. She would leave this house, this breeding ground for the conjurations of the augurous unseen, on the heels of Harold's having paid and gone.

The bath to a measure relaxed her tight nerves and she thought: This is the last one I'll have here. With each constraint of her toilet she thought it too: for the last time here.

She dressed with the suit in which she planned to travel and then, before going down to breakfast, stood for a while at a bedroom window observing the marshalling of the storm clouds across the sky. Shakespeare, during her drama courses, had used them so much. Symbols of darkest fate. Thunderous portents to underscore the pitfalls of the living. Sometimes of the dead.

Alfred Lord Tennyson had used them too: "Storm, such as drove her under moonless heavens till hard upon the cry of 'breakers' came the crash of ruin, and the loss of all—" The remembered passage erased the modest benefits of the bath from Clara's nerves. She shivered as though the battened cold had crept in from the outer air.

She paid Mrs. Porter after breakfast, and suggested that if Mrs. Porter would pack, Joe would drive her into town. No—no lunch. No dinner. Clara herself would throw something together. She wanted (Clara took a threadbare sideswipe at Garbo) just to be alone. With her dreams of tomorrow and, of course, of Robert Johnson.

As a matter of fact this sat all right with Mrs. Porter who, in spite of her passage through life with one of her feet in the grave, was as much a romanticist at heart as was Mrs. Lovestone.

While Mrs. Porter was upstairs Clara saw Joe in the living room. It was a curious scene of inner conflict for Clara, and her fingers were not quite steady as she paid him and thanked him both for his services, and for the use of his car. She added, as she had with Mrs. Porter, an extra month's pay, half expecting that he would refuse it, but he did not.

"Will you wait until Mrs. Porter is ready, and then drive her in, Joe?"

"I'll be glad to, Miss Carmandine."

Well, he would leave her now, and she would have the day in which to pack, and then alone, would face her rendezvous with Harold after the fall of night. A revulsion of her sleepless dreads, joined up with her reluctance to let Joe go, produced revolt. Her change of plan was instant, under the unsound, and reckless coercion of her nerves, and of her bootless hunger.

Clara ducked behind a willful blindness against the safe advisability that the place be empty for the meeting of Harold and herself. Her intended purpose to call a taxicab to drive her to the station once Harold would be gone was stashed.

Surely it could be done, what with Joe's quarters being above the garage, with a call system from the house, and she could ring or not according to how the moment would advise—Joe's strength, the fluid power of that body would be in waiting for her to loose at Harold in any variety of his purpose.

To copper this final bet.

He was looking at her curiously, waiting for dismissal, and she said: "Would you do me a favor, Joe? Tonight?" There was hesitancy in his echoed "Tonight?" and Clara, almost accepting it as one of her innumerable occult signs, said swiftly: "It's not important—not if you're tied up with anything, Joe."

"Just what time tonight, Miss Carmandine?"

"About eleven?"

His smile held pleased relief.

"Oh that will be fine. There's a bowling tournament I'm mixed up in, but whatever you want I can make it easily at that time."

She cut evasions.

"I've a business appointment at eleven. Could you be here by then, and would you wait in the garage until I ring?"

"Certainly."

"And then drive me to the station? I've decided to take the sleeper rather than the early morning train."

"I'll be glad to."

(How meager their talks had been, Clara thought. A slim package of repetitive certainties and I'll-be-glad-tos for her to remember.)

"And Joe—"

"Yes, Miss Carmandine?"

"I'm somewhat uncertain—I mean it might be necessary to have a witness signature on a document. So if I do ring the garage, would you come to the house at once? Will you surely come quickly, Joe?"

Joe said yes, while savoring experimentally the peculiar tension as it broke slender cracks in the enameled reserve with which he considered his employer to be coated. Nerves, yes, he knew she had spells of them, but it seemed nuts to think that she was actually afraid of something. Yet you couldn't quite help from feeling so. And in the name of common sense, what? She'd hooked a good rich guy and was marrying him tomorrow. The whole world was at her feet, in fact, to kick around as she wanted to.

Clara said in dismissal: "Then at eleven, Joe?"

"Yes, Miss Carmandine. Eleven."

CHAPTER 42

Noon came and over on Ashcourt Street Morris again walked up the stairs to Mrs. Lovestone's apartment. She was enchanted to see him.

He said: "I've had no luck. I hadn't heard from you. I happened to be passing by, so I just came up on a chance."

With active regret she told him that still no vacancy obtained—but surely he would have time for a cup of coffee?

Morris was absolutely positive that he would. They went into the living room. They sat. They sipped.

"Do you know, Mrs. Lovestone, I've not been able to get your remarkable story about coincidences out of my mind. It's like some tune that just keeps going around. How is your friend Miss Carmandine?"

Well, the dime was in the slot and the record began. Mrs. Lovestone gave a full description of the lavish coffee party of farewell at the Watertown house. She flushed romantically through the unexpected radiogram from Peru, the fact that Miss Carmandine was taking the night express to meet her fiancé at the flying field in New York tomorrow afternoon, the whole glorious, glorious climax to the Cinderella tale.

"Surely the radiogram must have come some days ago, Mrs. Lovestone? To give Miss Carmandine time to settle up about the house and things?"

"Yes—now let me see—yes, it was last Friday. She called me up, and told me almost as soon as she got it. I know it was Friday because of fish."

With an uneasy and unaccustomed sense of nervous tension Morris finished his coffee as conveniently as he could, and apologized for having to get back to the mills by one. He said goodbye, and hoped that there would be a message for him about a vacancy soon.

He drove to the telegraph office, and made inquiries.

No message of any nature had come through for a Miss Solda Carmandine on last Friday nor—the name was unusual—did the manager think there had been one at any other time.

Morris, returning to his office, felt uneasier still.

CHAPTER 43

Clara packed and saw to it that the upstairs rooms were in order. The suitcases were locked. Her hat and coat and gloves were in waiting on a chair.

She could not resist it. She counted the money again, spreading it on the smooth white counterpane of the bed, savoring its all but animate mint-new crispness. It was so wonderfully much, and would be multiplied by twice tonight. She gathered it up, and put it in a shoulder-strap bag—a style she detested but one which she had decided would be the least obvious, and most secure for the public transport of her loot.

Toward two o'clock Clara went downstairs, the shoulder-strap bag right with her, and telephoned the station for a drawing room on the sleeper. In the kitchen she put together a pickup lunch, and almost enjoyed eating it because of the wealth which was with her right under her hand.

Through the potential of its alchemy she was lolling on the golden strands of Bermuda, of Nassau, of Palm Beach, or underneath their successive moons (which accomplished the astronomical miracle of remaining constant at the full) while weaving around her were the scions of the important rich.

So bright were the golden turrets of this castle in Spain that their radiance befogged even Joe, and whatever Joe, or any Joe, might have stood for in her life. It was good, it was sensible and right to be tough, to get all you could from living, wring it dry, and wring dry all the people in it who would be overtaken along your golden path. Power, money, those were the firsts one lived for, for with them, later, she could shop around for love.

She washed the dishes, and put them away.

At three o'clock snow began to fall, and Clara turned on the ground-floor lights to repel the outer darkness of the storm. She moved irresponsibly from room to room, as nervous as a shut-in cat. The mirage of golden strands was gone, veiled darkly by forebodings of the coming night.

Artemus Simms, the real estate agent, stopped in at four, and Clara was glad of the break. He was such an absolute extrovert that it was impossible not to get an effect of tonic lift, or something, when you were with him.

He gamboled through the usual well-well-wells and what-weathers (but it hasn't put any crimp in *you*, Miss Carmandine, you look splendid) and then said: "It struck me that when you came in the other day I forgot to remind you about the telephone and lights. So many people when they leave unexpectedly—well, the bills just slip their minds."

"Mr. Simms, you're right. It frankly hadn't occurred to me—this last minute confusion—"

"Of course, of course. Well, your plans were so uncertain, Miss Carmandine—I mean they seem to cover so much territory—" (Ha-ha-ha) "—that any forwarding address seemed hardly practicable. I thought I'd just run out and remind you. It's a little late this afternoon, but you could take care of them in the morning."

"But I'm taking the sleeper tonight, Mr. Simms."

"You are? Well—let me see. Would you like to have me take care of them for you?"

"That would be awfully kind. Let me leave some money with you, say fifty dollars? I'm sure that will more than cover them."

Mr. Simms was, too. It was arranged, and in view of her taking the sleeper, would Miss Carmandine just leave the house keys under the door mat and he would pick them up tomorrow? He would also attend to shutting off the lights and water. When she and her imminent husband did settle down, if she would send him her address he would forward her a check for anything left over from the bills.

All this having been attended to, and the fifty tucked in his wallet, Mr. Simms said: "I trust your stay here has been pleasant, Miss Carmandine? Comfortable?"

"Completely so, Mr. Simms."

"Well," he said, casting a discreet eye upwards toward the attic—not that *he* believed in clanking chains or disembodied shrieks, of course, "I'm awfully glad of that." Snow and a taupe sedan swallowed Simms, and once more Clara was alone.

With little visual change the dark day blackened into night, and with night's falling the phantoms were at her again, and all the lamps of the living room were useless as spells to effect their exorcism.

At one moment Clara stood rigid in the center of the room. These, in her packing, she had forgot. Her eyes with deadly fascination moved from the miniature china dog on the mantel shelf to the sampler on the eastern wall, to the sweet grass sewing basket on the table beside an armchair.

Backward through time they again transported Solda.

(How *truly* lovely the water is, Clara—there's a pond on the farm, but it's only knee deep and stagnant sort of, and Papa uses it for the ducks to swim in. I remember one time, it was in summer, Clara, just like now—)

"Stop it! Stop it!" Clara found herself saying fiercely, aloud to the china dog.

She moved swiftly to the table, and snatched up the shoulder-strap bag, hugging tight against her breast her lovely money until she was no longer shaking, and Solda was receding into that vortex which has no determination nor an end.

Harold misted into Solda's place, while the hours passed—seven o'clock—eight—nine—and a crescendoing review of Clara's pros and cons covering the advantages and disadvantages for Harold if, instead of handing over the balance of the money, he killed her.

CHAPTER 44

Under the fluorescent overheads of Mickey's Pastime and Athletic Club Joe's bowling ball struck with a clash, a breath, a wobble, and the tenth pin joined its fellows for a strike.

"That," said Frank, his partner on their two-man team, "sews it up. Let's get us some beers."

"What's the time?"

"Why the time?"

"I've got a job still to do tonight."

"Okay, so let's have some beer."

"All right."

In the sedate and handsome library of the Witherspoon Club Harold, in a state of tremendous nervous tension, gave up any pretence of reading his book. He looked at his watch. It was stupid to have set an appointed time. It simply magnified the moment into a tenser importance. Like the exact hour on which a historic document was to be signed, or the precise second for the switch during an electrocution.

Old Biggerly paused by Iris chair, and said with his usual senile whinny: "Taking a night off, Davis?" Harold gave a nervous start.

"No—no," he said. "I was just deciding to go home." Biggerly heh-hehd away, and Harold stood up. He put the book back in its proper place on the shelf. Absently he considered Biggerly, and other specimens of advanced second childhood.

Childhood—

He left the room.

From a drugstore Morris telephoned his house and said to Freda: "I may not be back for quite a while, Freda. Don't wait up for me."

"All right, Walter. There'll be sandwiches in the ice box."

"And beer?"

"And beer."

"Good night, now."

"Good night, Walter."

Morris went out, and sat behind the wheel of his car.

He did not start it. The lazy aimlessness of the town drifted sparsely by. The snow dropped in dark tears against a street lamp. Far over in the distance, where the railroad lay, a whistle wailed. He pulled up the collar of his overcoat.

He felt cold.

CHAPTER 45

While the rale of the wind droned its morbid gusts against them, Clara bolted windows and drew down their shades. The hands of the clock stood at half past nine.

She locked the front door, and the kitchen door, and returning to the living room was foundered by a feeling of futility, that the locking and bolting of things was a gesture which had accomplished nothing beyond entombing herself with her miserable thoughts during the one and a half more hours which faced her until eleven. And until the tough, strong sanctuary of Joe.

Joe would come all right. He wouldn't let her down. Even under the spell and competition of bowling he wouldn't let her down, he'd keep track of the time. She compelled herself to believe that this fact was true.

Her mind in its rising fever swung to money, not her own big, wonderful lot of money, but the extra month's pay for Joe. It would have been sort of nice if he hadn't taken it, as if he had, in a way, liked doing things for her herself, instead of only doing things for her, for the money he got out of it.

She would then, Clara decided, have, given him a handsome and expensive present. She was too nerved up to consider that she wouldn't have been here to buy him one, nor that later with safety could she send him one. Well, why shouldn't he be out for money? She was. She'd got money. The word started somersaults in her brain.

The doorbell rang at ten.

Clara snapped into immobility from her restless pacing as though a curb bit had levered her with cruel force. Only her eyes moved toward the clock, and they assured her she was not mistaken in the hour. Her torturous mind, with its interminable schemings, plunged into a welter of possibilities each one of which yelled danger.

And each one of which focused smack on Harold.

She was beyond any shred of conservative reasoning on the point: had Harold come early? Had he done this purposely, perhaps divining (Clara surged right along with the tide of her fright, without remotely treading water to figure out through what occult powers Harold could have concluded this) that she might have some guard—Joe—on hand at eleven for her protection?

Was he here now to kill her?

Was he here now to pay the balance of the money and so bring the deal to a mutually satisfactory close?

The doorbell rang again.

Clara refused to risk it. Let Harold come back. Never would she unlock the door until the appointed hour came and, with it, the bodyguard strength of Joe.

She stood breathing shallowly in the tremulous stillness which held no sound beyond that of the tireless wind in its baffled passage through the pines.

A little crash further impinged on the stillness, and then the tinkle of falling glass on the hardwood of the hall floor.

Clara's mental image of the front door's fanlight was swift, its fanlight with the repeated glass tracery of its pattern carried in narrow oblongs down on either side of the door.

With steps over which she had no conscious control Clara walked out into the hallway. A coarse-gloved hand was careful through jagged glass, and its fingers were closed on the key. They were turning the key.

The door opened, and slammed shut against a swirl of driven snow. A man was in the hallway, locking the door again. He pocketed the key.

With her body cold, and bloodless, and straight on the edge of hitting the violent shakes, Clara observed the stranger while the notion trickled around, like slow molasses, that he was a thug whom Harold had hired to kill her. In this deadly grip of bitter cold she lazied toward the disgusted conclusion that she might have known Harold never would have had the nerve to pull the job himself.

For an appreciable while the man stood observing her with steady, peculiar eyes. Then he shook snow from the shoulders of his coat and slapped a good deal of it from the brim of his hat.

He said in a voice strangely quiet in contrast to his brutish hulk: "Have you no welcome for your Papa, Solda?"

So—it was Solda's father, Antonio Carmandine. Relief tumbled over Clara in a flood, and she rode with it effortlessly. Her veins had blood again, and her lungs felt strong.

In the heady release of this not being a murderous Harold, Clara gripped at the lifebelt (for in her feverish thoughts the ultimate eventuality of a lethal Harold did not subside) of throwing herself into the role of Solda to the hilt. At all costs, she felt, she must keep Carmandine with her as a protector—her belief for the need of this still strongly persisted—until Joe would take over at eleven.

Careful—Clara swiftly marshaled all of the things which Solda had said through that hot and lazy afternoon, and through the twilight: things weren't too friendly between her father and Solda—the bitter curse he had put upon her when she had left the farm—the drudgery of her childhood—the slow burnings of his temper, with their unpredictable flares of terrific rage which would leave Solda weak and sick—no, this was no loving meeting of father and child, the role called for a guarded reserve—

"Give me your coat and hat, Papa."

"Well, now. That is a little better."

Carmandine tugged his feral arms from the sheepskin lining of a heavy coat, releasing a waft of animal at Clara when she took it.

"How did you know I lived here, Papa?"

"That gibbering old idiot where you lived before, Solda. She told me in her letters. She told me all about you.

Clara could well imagine, and so that was it: Carmandine had traveled east to gouge what he could from his daughter's Lovestone-publicized good fortune. And that was fine. It gave Clara the upper hand. She would string him along until Joe came. She would tell him what room to stay in when Harold came. And if (her optimism under the flush of an at-hand protector cycled at once to high) all went all right with Harold she would just drive off with Joe and leave Solda's father in the room where she had put him.

Even if he should stay and, tomorrow, Mr. Simms would find him, what would it matter? Solda had simply evaded her father, had deliberately left him there to get away from him, and had slipped off into her brilliant future and private life.

Yes, she thought, things indeed were turning out very smooth and sweet.

"I will make you some coffee, Papa. There is nothing else to offer except a little bread. I am going away tonight on the train, so the house is practically shut up."

"Yes, I know." (It did not occur to Clara to wonder how Carmandine knew this. She was too intent on sinking herself in the role of Solda.) "I do not want any coffee. I am not hungry."

"Come in here, Papa, and we will sit down."

Clara led the way into the living room, distastefully conscious of the animalistic emanation from Carmandine who was so very close behind her, while the word jungles slipped across her thoughts and was gone.

"This room, it has cost a lot of money, Solda?"

"Yes, Papa, but the things are not mine. They were bought by the man who owns the house and who went west last year."

"He is rich, yes?"

"I guess so, Papa. I know nothing about him at all." Clara wished that Carmandine would settle, instead of going on with the slow survey he was making of the room. She considered this chitchat about Watertown's probable richness simply as a build-up to a sound questioning about her own new richness.

"Do let's sit down, Papa."

Carmandine sat, with a warily poised effect, in an armchair and Clara put it down (he seemed in a fashion to be *coiled*, really) to ill ease in the face of his daughter's changed financial status in life, and the consequent deference he would feel he would now have to show her. She considered how galling for a tyrant of his nature it must be.

"You are going away on the train to meet *him*, to meet this Johnson fellow, Solda?"

"Yes, Papa."

"You are not married yet?"

"No."

"Ah."

It was more than a sigh. It amounted to the release of a breath which had been held in overlong. Not since that initial observation in the hall had he looked at her directly until this minute, rather his eyes had been segments of hot black buttons under half-lowered, thick-lashed fids.

He must have hated Solda very much, Clara thought, for the first time really consciously noting his eyes and getting a pretty definite appreciation of their savage implacability, while the word jungle once more slid through her head. But, because it was Solda he hated, the matter did not affect her.

What under the sun was it one talked about in Bethel? What served as the casual banalities of social use? Probably the same as everywhere else, she supposed. The weather.

"This wind has been blowing all day, Papa."

"Yes, and the snow too. It is heavy and thick and banking up even among the pines."

The remark showed a curiously pointed familiarity with the grounds, especially in the sense of a perception acquired after simply reaching here in the obscurity of a pitch-dark night.

More than just darkness, Clara thought, for there were the snow, and cold, and a whine in the steady wind, and the cold crept insinuatingly back within her too.

"How would you know about the pines, Papa?"

"Because I have been among them all day."

This made no sense. Clara subscribed to the fairly general misconception that the majority of people who lived on farms went crazy, just as each village had its idiot, and she wondered whether Carmandine could be touched. A sidelong glance at the clock showed a full fifty minutes left before she could expect Joe.

"Why did you do that, Papa? Why didn't you let me know you were here?"

"Because I wanted to have you all by myself, Solda." Carmandine again was not looking at her directly, but letting the black bits of his shielded eyes slide just alongside of her.

A halting sprout of fright caused Clara to say: "What makes you think we are alone here now?"

Carmandine gestured expansively, his powerful arms spread wide in a patient shrug, and his thick steel-strong fingers were prehensile in their waiting.

"After the man and the woman drove off with their bags I saw you pass an upstairs window. I came in."

"You were here—inside the house?"

He said with a flare of arrogant impatience: "Yes, I am a clever man, Solda. I have an intelligence that is big. It is much, much bigger than you have ever given me credit for. While you were upstairs packing I took my time and looked around. There was nobody else in the house then but myself and you. I left as you were coming downstairs, and I have concerned myself with observations from my position among the pines."

"All day—Papa—"

He continued to be absorbed with his own priceless cleverness which unquestionably, with the passage of years, had developed into an active form of megalomania.

"That man who came in the afternoon was soon gone. And nobody else has come since. I did not choose to use the daylight hours. The night is better for my purpose. I have waited until this late, little Solda, to make sure that there will be nobody here but you and me."

Where was this leading to? Why was her skin so cold again? Clara, with a revulsion which stabbed her sharply, altered her opinion of Carmandine, translating him from a welcome source of protection into a—what? The shoulder bag with all its beautiful money, tucked beside her on the chair—did he know? Would he seize it from her, and go? What against that bulk of strength could she do? What in *any* instance could she do?

"I have had—I am sure that Mrs. Lovestone must have written you about it—I have had some good fortune, Papa. Of course you will understand she is a woman who has no sense of proportion about things? You would laugh if you knew how greatly she exaggerates. I'll tell you—when I am married you must let me send a nice big present to you? Something you will—truly like—Papa."

Carmandine was up and hugely over her, all in one smooth move which you could scarcely catch before it was done. The calloused emery of his palm slapped viciously across her lips, and the lower one welled instant drops of blood. His hands settled on the arms of her chair pinning her in, and as he stood bending close, the animal smell exuded in waves each time he breathed.

He said: "Enough!"

Clara's tongue experimentally tasted the sickish salt of blood, and she was going to scream, going to let out that jammed-up ice block in her stomach, and scream, and his right hand slowly left the arm of the chair, and she did not.

"Don't hit me again," Clara said, or she was pretty sure she said it. "Go away."

The full anarchy of Carmandine's temper and irritability spewed out. His delusions of grandeur (which had been indicated so pointedly in his handwriting, if Mrs. Lovestone had had even the barest nodding acquaintanceship with graphology) pyramided him into a virtual spitting of the brilliance which, to his own perfect satisfaction, set him apart as a rarity among men.

He gave it to this simple creature in the plainest language so that she would both understand, and would appropriately suffer, and as to why he wished her to suffer he would explain in sufficient detail when it pleased him to get around to it.

In a sentence: the fortune which on the authority of Mrs. Lovestone's letter Solda now had in her personal possession and right, would go to her father in his role of next of kin, if Solda were to die before she had married Johnson.

Quite conversationally Carmandine added that his purpose in coming east and in being here now was to kill her.

He stood back from the chair at last and breathed deeply in his pleasure. He watched for things to chase across her face, like horror, like sometimes how your dog would look when he knew he was in for it. He followed with interest a blood drop hesitating, and then dripping from her chin.

"And what have you got to say to me, Solda?"

It took care, and time, and effort to get the words out straight. There was no other avenue open beyond instantly shedding this masquerade. What future perils, what ruin of all her plans and hopes this might entail were no longer of the vaguest consequence. The murder urge of this crazy monster, for Clara knew now that he was crazy, must be quenched.

"I am not Solda."

This jounced Carmandine into a momentary astonishment. Then the very audacity, the very impudence of this puling wretch attempting to pull such a febrile absurdity on, of all men him, touched a hotter flame to the smoulder of his temper.

"And what now is this?"

"I am not Solda, Mr. Carmandine. I'm Clara Davis."

The name stirred sluggishly in his memory.

The clock had leisurely moved its hands to half past ten.

Davis—Clara Davis—Carmandine had it now.

"That too was in that old fool's letters. That name of Clara Davis. She is dead. She was drowned a couple of months ago." He added reasonably: "Why do you make such an idiot of yourself, Solda?"

Her lip, Clara thought, was already swelling. It felt puffy. A wave of torpor through her terror caused the lip to worry her more than her inability, which she fully realized, to convince this man, other than by her bare word, that she, Clara, was living and that his daughter was in her grave.

Only Solda wasn't in her grave when you looked at it obliquely, say from Mr. Carmandine's point of view—or, she wondered as a chill, that was like no earthly chill, washed her heart, could it be from any point of view? *Were* there such things, things beyond the province of plain dreams, thin unseen hosts forever—unheld by earth or stones—

"I am Clara Davis. I'm not your daughter." Carmandine went to the mantel shelf and picked up the miniature china dog. His voice held all the danger of being perfectly composed.

"From your best friend Elsie Strumson on your seventh birthday. Is it not so, Solda?"

The souvenir shattered into infinite fragments from the force with which Carmandine hurled it against the hearth. He derived a huge satisfaction from this modest breakage, almost as though it were a spiced hors d'oeuvre to whet his appetite for the lustier courses to come.

Gripped in a sweeping exhibitionism of sadistic delight Carmandine spattered against this sad seated object, his daughter, the gall of distaste which had poisoned his breast through the years, his strong and capacious breast which he pummeled in emphasis with mallet fists.

A furious economy served as a carrying strain for his invective: the invalidism of Mama after Solda's birth, and of what use to do a woman's work was an invalid Mama? No. Money, precious money had had to be paid for a woman to attend to the picayune details of the farmhouse, to say nothing of an infuriatingly lingering mama, and this for seven expensive years, until Solda was grown enough to take over.

Then what.

When on Solda's eighteenth birthday Mama had died, and Mama's money had been given Solda by the bank, had she repaid the care and keep which he had lavished on her, and which, in the name of the commonest justice, he had had every reason to expect?

Carmandine paused to permit this atrocity (he did not bother to review her betrayal, her wicked clinging to this cash of Mama's nor her profligate, vicious, hell-inspired desertion of her comfortable home) to sink in, while the clock's minute hand dallied its coursing towards the hour at twenty-five.

He lowered his voice to the dramatic register of a whisper.

"And so you tell me that you are not Solda!"

He was back on this note again, amply infuriated both by its outrageous falsity and the even more dastardly assumption on Solda's part that he, Carmandine, would be such a chump as to swallow it. With a sweep his hand sent Mama's sweet grass sewing basket hurtling to join the china fragments on the hearth.

"I suppose you can cook up a few more lies, and tell me how anybody else could have these things but you, Solda?"

The sailboat sampler occupied him next, and he read aloud with fine sarcasm its kindly, gentle words: "'He maketh the storm a calm, so that the waves thereof are still—'"

He reached over, and tore the sampler from the wall, crushing its cloth and cardboard backing, and its cheap strip of frame, into a compact wad, with the pleased anticipation of hurling it in Solda's face.

But when he turned around again Solda was gone.

CHAPTER 46

At the well-packed bar of Mickey's Pastime and Athletic Club Frank said: "Another beer, Joe?"

"No, Frank. I'd better shove. I told Miss Carmandine I'd be back at eleven."

"Nuts, you can step on it. What difference will a few minutes make—one way or the other?"

"Probably none, but she's got the wind up about something."

"About what?"

"I don't know. I guess I'd better shove. Even now, with this storm, there's just about an even chance that I can make it."

"Well, be seeing you, Joe."

"Be seeing you."

At the far less packed, and much sedater bar of the Witherspoon Club Harold finished his highball, signed the slip, and said to Mike, the bartender: "Time to go home."

"Goodnight, Mr. Davis."

"Goodnight, Mike."

"Watch the roads. They say they're not so hot."

"I will."

Harold got his coat and hat and went out to his car. Traffic, because of the storm, was light. Even if I don't drive too fast, he thought, I guess I can make it all right.

Morris pressed the starter of his car. He pulled away from the curb.

He thought: Well, this will wrap it up.

And yet, although the heater was on full, he still felt chill.

CHAPTER 47

Carmandine watched Clara jump down from the kitchen porch. It amused him inordinately to let her struggle for a distance through piling drifts into the sting of blinding snow, while the scarlet enameling of her nails groped despairingly toward the black sanctuary of night. Then he was softly and quietly after her.

He bundled her beneath an arm and dropped her on the kitchen floor, while he locked its door and pocketed the key.

She was at the telephone when he turned. He slapped it from her hand. He stooped and yanked its cord from the baseboard box, and Clara was away again but this did not bother him.

Where could she go?

The only two doors downstairs were locked, and an unhurried tour of the rooms showed Carmandine emptiness, and windows still fastened down with their bolts. If she were to throw herself from an upstairs one she would be stunned. Most probably she would break something, and then he could take his time and break the rest of her.

Carmandine walked with the poise of an oversized panther up the stairs.

The stealth of dual treads continued: the quiet expedition of his stalking, and Clara's amateur charade toward flight, with both unheard beneath the endless susurrus of wind.

With finical patience, Carmandine turned on their lights, and examined every room, their cupboards, and even under their beds. Empty, all was emptiness. He located the attic stairs, and leaving the well-lighted hallway, moved catlike up their darkness into the still darker chamber above.

He stood still at the head of them in the inky pall while the wind slid with more impatient whispers over the surface of the close-by roof. He would have liked to have heard her breathe, but because of the wind sounds he could not. It was a small wish, and did not matter.

His blunt, curved fingers reached like sensitive antennae into the black, testing its obstacles as he gently moved, loving this game, loving it to its littlest drop. The fingertips brushed wood which Carmandine identified as the back of a chair. He tilted the chair deliberately, and let it fall back on the floor with a smack which, in this ghosted vault, held the shock of a shot.

A whimpered, wettish scream made him smile. Cloth brushed against him but he did not move, not until against the less dark oblong of the attic door, he saw her in shaking silhouette start creeping down the stairs.

He was not far behind, and with now blooding eyes he watched her keep creeping on along the hallway, and down the stairway, with her red nails desperate upon its rail, in heaven knew what absurd expectations of escape in this wilted creeping towards the locked front door. Like the perfectly senseless and lethargically urgent movements (which always absorbed him) of a mortally shot animal who keeps right on wanting to live.

He let her fingers touch the door. He let them fumble with its knob, and then he took her in his arms.

The ultimate of horror came to Clara as, with gentleness, the pressure started its application against her ribs.

"Nobody knows that I have come here," Carmandine's breath said. "Nobody will see me go."

The gentleness began to leave the pressure and a touch of firmness took its place.

"I will be waiting on the farm for the news of your death, Solda," the breath said.

(*And Solda said in the waters of the moonlit river: Why, it's lovely. Like floating on air—Clara!—Clara—Cla—bubbles and a little thrashing and bubbles—no bubbles—*)

The slow approach to death began for Clara, and pain got even more unendurable than terror, as the arms of this huge evil force enjoyed the little-by-little accession of their pressing. Her lungs, in their cruel congestion, felt much like Solda's must have felt as the clock tinkled prettily into chiming eleven times, and Clara was dead.

Carmandine did not let her go. Her empty body was listless in his arms as he stood with it, sated and bestial, his whole being drugged into an immobile stupor from the accomplishment of his imponderable hatred of this sleazy rag, all gutted of the lust to kill.

The smallest of his catalogue of muscles did not stir, while the lock of the door was shot out, nor while Morris and Joe closed in upon both him and the object that had been Clara, and which did not slump until the butt of Morris's gun crushed hard against Carmandine's skull.

"There isn't any use," Morris said.

Joe stood up from kneeling beside Clara. Even his lips were very white.

"So that's what she was afraid of," he said.

Morris looked at Joe curiously.

"So it seems."

"Wonder who he is."

Morris fished out a wallet from the stertorously-breathing Carmandine's pants pocket. He looked at a driver's license.

"Antonio Carmandine, Bethel, Minnesota."

"Her father."

"So," Morris repeated, "it seems."

"You never can get used to it," Joe said, looking at the loose-boned Clara. "Saw plenty of it in the Bulge, but you never can get used to it. Anyhow, not like this."

Morris located the telephone in the kitchen. He came back to Joe.

"He ripped the phone out. Do something for me, will you?"

"Certainly Sergeant."

"Take a run in your car to the nearest place that's open and telephone the dope on this to headquarters, will you? Maybe it would be just as quick if you went there direct. Not," Morris added, "that there's any hurry. Not now."

He waited until he heard the sound of Joe's car. He turned Carmandine over on his stomach and pulling back his arms fastened his wrists with handcuffs. He took a tablecloth from the dining room and arranged it over Clara.

He went outside.

CHAPTER 48

Morris found him being wretchedly sick beneath the pines.

"Better go sit down in your car, Mr. Davis," Morris said. "Need any help?"

"No," Harold said after a moment, "I'm quite all right now. It was weak—impardonably weak of me—"

"Don't even think about it. Plenty of men, very tough men, get sick when they face up against a sight as bad as that was."

They trudged through snow, leaning against iced wind.

"I saw, of course, that there was a car which kept ahead of me after leaving the outskirts of the town, and then I also knew that one was following me. Yours, Sergeant Morris."

"I've been following you quite a lot, Mr. Davis."

"When the car ahead turned in here I backed off the road under the pines. I wanted to wait until the man was gone, but you went right on, and joined him on the porch, and after you shot the lock out, I went up and looked and, well, I just got terribly sick."

Morris held the front door of Harold's car open.

"Get in and sit down, Mr. Davis."

"Thank you."

"I haven't got much time to talk, so you just listen. First off, there is very little about this business that I don't know right now, and what that little is I will get from you. I give the boys about a half an hour before they get here. Will you do just what I tell you to, Mr. Davis?"

"Of course, but I don't quite understand—"

"At the minute you don't need to. Tomorrow morning I would like to see you at ten."

"Certainly—I'll be at your office—"

"No, I think it will be wiser if we make it at your camp. Have you used it at all since the drowning?"

"No, neither I nor Edna—neither of us felt—"

"That is what I thought."

"I'm frankly bewildered, Sergeant Morris, and I don't know how I could ever—I mean my having practically been a witness, and your not insisting that I stay—"

"Tomorrow at your camp at ten. Shove off, Mr. Davis—and take it easy on these roads. You've got lots of time."

Harold did drive slowly for he was a thoroughly shaken man. His nerves were all but completely gone. It seemed incredible to him that he would not become publicly involved. He could not, with the faintest acceptance of reason, plumb the position which Morris, if tonight were any criterion, seemed preparing to take.

The thought of a possible shakedown was instantly dismissed. Never, not by a man like Morris.

He was well within the town limits when a couple of police cars sirened past. They were followed, without siren, by Joe. Just before he turned into the country club road an ambulance sirened by, in swift pursuit of the cars already gone.

That will be for Clara, Harold thought, and possibly for that man, whoever he was, who had killed her. He was glad to see that the downstairs lights were out when he reached home. He put the car in the garage, and saw as he walked back to the house, that the lights in Edna's rooms were still on.

He had lost all sense of, or interest in, time and was astonished to see, by the luminous hands of his wrist watch, that it was just twenty minutes before midnight.

The hallway was warm and comfortably dim with its low-wattage night bulb. He put his things in the coat-room and went slowly upstairs. He could not honestly remember ever having been so dreadfully tired, not tired exactly, rather it was like being drained right out, and having nothing left but a brittle, nervous shell.

Edna's living room door opened as he neared it, and he saw that she was still in a dinner dress.

"I heard the car on the gravel, Harold. How was the game?"

"Fine, Edna."

"I've sandwiches and milk. Why not mix a highball and tell me about it?"

"I—think if you don't mind I'll turn right in. Driving back through the snow was sort of a strain. There's quite a storm out, you know."

"It did seem, from the window, as though it were snowing very hard. By all means do go right to bed, dear." She kissed him. "Good night, Harold."

"Good night, Edna."

In his own rooms Harold took packets of hundred-dollar bills from several pockets, and placed them in a small dresser drawer. From the hip pocket of his trousers he took a .22-caliber automatic which he had owned since his days in college. He put it in with the money, and shut the drawer.

It wasn't over-warm in the room, and yet he found himself sweating. He thought it was because of the question which would always be with him, of whether it might have been the money or the gun, and the answer to which even he would never know.

CHAPTER 49

The morning edition of the *Gazette* had the story on the streets (with a shriek of seventy-two point headlines) by seven o'clock.

It had been a busy night not only for the gentlemen of the press, but for Artemus Simms, for Joe, for Mrs. Porter and Mrs. Lovestone as well.

The grist ground by the *Gazette* from Simms was small. Miss Carmandine had said nothing of her past, and little of her future beyond that she wanted a quiet place in which to stay until her fiancé returned from Peru—and boy, poor woman, did she find it!

The only reference she had given Simms was a Mrs. Adelia Lovestone on Ashcourt Street. Miss Carmandine seemed to have plenty of money, and had paid in cash. Yes, that had seemed a little odd but Simms had been only too glad to get the Watertown place off his books, under any circumstances. After this lead, the attic suicide by clothesline of Mr. Watertown was promptly exhumed from the *Gazette*s morgue, and heartily rehashed.

Both Joe and Mrs. Porter were on the meager side too, when it came to shedding any definitely factual light on Clara. Both of them held the common ground that Miss Carmandine had at times struck them as being nervous and, particularly during the past two weeks, as being downright afraid.

No, not to either of them had she ever said a word as to this fear's possible cause. Naturally it was perfectly obvious that a dread of her father lay at the bottom of it.

What else? He killed her, didn't he?

But Mrs. Lovestone was a rich, lush field. The *Gazette* turned loose their sob sister, Louella Larke (she kept pets, not cats, just a minor circus of spinning white mice) and under her practiced guidance, Mrs. Lovestone did not stint.

The story of Solda emerged from her fluid lips in the full panoply of its romantic and jewel-encrusted dazzle, as did Mrs. Lovestone's vivid opinion of that bestial parental brute who had murdered her. It was greatly regretted that Carmandine's muddied and scrabbled letter had been burned, but Miss Larke understood *so* well just how Mrs. Lovestone had felt about it, and would Mrs. Lovestone try to remember what had been in it, the very exact words?

As if she could forget! Mrs. Lovestone soared through the epistle in jig time—the *Gazette* boxed it under the headline: Premeditation Implied.

Concerning the glamorous and wealthy Robert Johnson there was a considerable to-do. Long distance telephone calls to the inter-American airlines, radio telephone calls to the United States consuls in Peru, further calls to the morgues of the Philadelphia and New York City newspapers, all proved to the *Gazette*'s, and the police department's, satisfaction that Solda's fiancé did not, and never had existed.

This also Mrs. Lovestone was perfectly well able to explain to Louella Larke. Mr. Johnson had been either a figment of Solda's romantic imagination—or (and would Miss Larke please keep this sotto voce? Oh yes Miss Larke would!) he had simply been a beast, like all men, one who veiled his evil intentions behind an alias, and who gave Solda the money she had turned up with, in payment for you-know-what. Solda, should such have been the circumstances, being now translated into a broken blossom, one bruised beneath the heartless heels of man. Even Miss Larke's pencil almost tripped over itself.

But there was, Miss Larke explained, no money. None, that was, to speak of. There were a hundred and twenty dollars, and some silver, in Miss Carmandine's purse, and her father, when searched in jail, produced little more than thirty dollars in bills and change.

This was a bad blow to Mrs. Lovestone, as her thoughts had already been busied with an elaborate funeral, and with herself under full sail as *entrepreneur des pompes funèbre*. She said so to Miss Larke, who smiled astutely and told her not to worry.

By the time she (Miss Larke) got through with Solda Carmandine there wouldn't be a dry female eye in town. There was no question whatever, but that the *Gazette* would start a fund, and that subscriptions would pour in.

Solda Carmandine would be buried magnificently in the cemetery here in Blush Falls or, should any up-popping relatives insist on the job being done in Minnesota, her remains, elaborately casketed, would magnificently be escorted to the train.

"But first will she lie in state, Miss Larke?"

"Miss Lovestone, in absolute state."

CHAPTER 50

Harold reached the camp at exactly ten. He found the front door unlocked, and Morris already inside.

"I hope you don't mind, Mr. Davis. I've keys for such things. I've been here before."

"No, of course not, Sergeant Morris. It's quite all right. Useless sort of things, locks, anyway."

"Very useless."

It was the beginning of a strange interview, and one which Morris said must remain completely off the record. There was a touch of restraint, and a certain embarrassment over both of them.

The police, Moms said, were satisfied, and for them the case was closed. Carmandine had been caught red-handed in the murder of his daughter. He had made no trouble at all, when taken to jail, about giving and signing a statement which even included his premeditation of the crime.

"It was factual down to the least detail, Mr. Davis, and will meet no opposition in court. He absolutely enjoyed giving them, and his only worry was his wanting to be quite sure he had done a good job, that Miss Carmandine positively was dead. They reassured him that she was."

Even the lawyer who had been directed to defend him had privately admitted to the district attorney that his contact with the case would simply be that of a figurehead required by the law.

Carmandine was cooked.

There was this about justice, Morris said. The main thing, as Morris saw it, was that it be truly done. Take now, Clara Davis. She had murdered Solda Carmandine for profit, and she had paid for her crime as fully, if not perhaps more fully, than she would have under the penalty of the State. Carmandine, with premeditation, had murdered his own flesh and blood, for so he was convinced she was, and he would pay the ultimate penalty too.

Well, that all in Morris's opinion stacked up to pretty good justice.

"Would you tell me, Mr. Davis, exactly what Clara Davis was after? I can guess the main outline all right, but I'd like to have the story from you."

Harold told him.

"Well, there you are," Morris said.

He expressed with moderation his good opinion of Harold, and of Edna, and of their decent way of life. If to disrupt their lives, for no conceivable use, would serve the technicalities of justice, then Morris wanted no part of it.

"You're in the clear right now, Mr. Davis, and I want you to stay that way. Joe was too horrified with what he saw through the glass to know anything about your being out at the Watertown place last night. Nobody knows you were there but me."

There was nothing, Harold felt, that he could say, nor anything really that he could do for Morris, beyond the deepest and most heartfelt job of thanking him. He hoped earnestly that maybe, in time, he could think up something he could do.

Morris felt this, and went on to give a little digest of his initial interest in the case.

"I didn't quite like the fact of the body's fingertips being abraded— so badly that there wasn't a chance of making identification positive by getting prints, and comparing them with objects your wife had handled around the house. It could have happened just as the boys thought, but it could also have been contrived."

"I—suppose it was, of course?"

"Contrived? Oh yes, like all of the job was contrived. Take a look around you here. It's one of the reasons I suggested the camp, so you could see for yourself, as well as for privacy."

"It looks perfectly all right to me. I mean there aren't any signs of disorder—struggle, things like that?"

"It is too perfectly all right, Mr. Davis, and that is what was the trouble with it. Suppose, as Clara Davis wanted us to assume, she came here alone, took off her clothes, and went in for a midnight swim and drowned."

"Well?"

"Well, where are the clothes?"

"Yes—of course—Clara couldn't, being drowned, have come back, and either put them away or got rid of them."

"That's right. It's about the only stupid thing she did. She should have dressed right here in Solda Carmandine's clothes, and left her own scattered around wherever it was she dropped them when she took them off for the swim."

"But the rest of the investigating force, Sergeant Morris—hadn't that also occurred to them."

"Look, Mr. Davis, you do not know the police. I don't say that if there had been any initial doubt whatever about the case they wouldn't have been onto this like hot cakes. They would have. But there wasn't. It was a straight accidental drowning, and you positively identified the body."

"But you, Sergeant Morris, how was it that you said nothing?"

Morris had known that this would come, and was hotly uncomfortable.

"You told me that you took a run out here the morning after she disappeared. You said you just looked inside and saw the place was empty, that you touched nothing. Well, you might have touched a lot. Amateurs always go way off the beam in trying to cover up."

"You thought I might have killed Clara?"

"Sure, Mr. Davis. Naturally I did. But what had I actually to go on? Nothing, when you came right down to it. I kept my trap shut, and went after it my own way. The rest of the boys were perfectly happy. I don't need to say now that I'm glad things are as they are."

"I'll be indebted to you for as long as I live, I think. And Edna will too."

Morris tugged an oblong package from the pocket of his overcoat.

"Count this when you get home," he said. "It's yours. I got it from her shoulder-strap bag before the boys came."

While Harold and Morris were driving to their homes, the waiter at Blancharde's was wearily bemused with the picture of the murdered Solda Carmandine in the *Gazette*.

He said to the bartender: "I got it now. Them dames were here together."

"What dames, and when?"

"How would I know? Give me a beer."

The brief episode was the minutest pin point in time, but it did remove the final shadow from the future course of Harold's life.

It was of course inexpressible, the relief which as the car rolled on toward home, Harold felt.

Edna said to him at luncheon: "The drive did you a world of good, dear. You look like another man."

"I feel like one."

"I was worried about you, Harold."

"Well, you mustn't, Edna. There isn't a thing."

Edna caught the present tense, and added it to the links of her private thoughts. To the principal link above all others: the startling resemblance between the picture in this morning's *Gazette* of Miss Carmandine and Clara. To Harold's several absences with their poor, dear excuses. To the locket which had been his mother's, and which she had come across under his handkerchiefs when she had straightened out the drawer.

With the infinite wisdom of all fine women toward one whom they truly love Edna simply asked him whether he would like more salmon, and Harold said that his appetite seemed on the mark again and that he would.

CHAPTER 51

The funeral of Solda Carmandine was one of the better successes ever pulled off by Blush Falls.

No relatives from Minnesota had popped up, in fact nobody had cared very much where she was buried, with the exception of Mrs. Lovestone who, in tow of Louella Larke and a *Gazette* camera man, personally picked out the plot in the cemetery, where the view was pleasant toward the river and the hills.

The contributions to the *Gazette* fund had totaled an amazing list of small amounts, and had included one especially amazing donation, because of its size, from an anonymous donor.

Almost everybody went, and Harold from an elevation which gave a good view of the grave, was joined by Morris.

"Do you know," Harold said, "that during my talk with Clara about what it would be best for us to do she actually mentioned Enoch Arden? I can't help thinking about it. Are you familiar with the poem, Sergeant Morris?"

"Yes, and I've also thought she was pretty familiar with it too."

"Well, take right now. Of course it's a terrible travesty, a sort of a horrible distortion of Tennyson's intent—but are you familiar with the final stanza?"

"No, Mr. Davis, not literally."

"It runs like this," Harold said. "'So past the strong heroic soul away. And when they buried him the little port had seldom seen a costlier funeral.'"

Earth fell on Clara.

And then everybody went away.

ABOUT RUFUS KING

Rufus King (1893–1966) was an American author of Whodunit crime novels. He created four series of detective stories: the first one with Reginald De Puyster, a sophisticated detective similar to Philo Vance; the second one with his more famous character, Lieutenant Valcour; Colin Starr, who appeared in four stories in the *Strand Magazine* during 1940/41; and Detective Bill Duggan, who appeared in three stories in 1956/57. The Bill Duggan stories include his most famous short work, "Malice in Wonderland" (which loaned its title to his 1958 hardcover short story collection).

Modern critics are rediscovering Rufus King's work. Mike Grost, on *Golden Age Detective*, features a long writeup of King, stating: "King had a vivid writing style, with colorful characters, events, and images. He was clearly a born writer."

www.ingramcontent.com/pod-product-compliance
Lightning Source LLC
Chambersburg PA
CBHW020136180626
46810CB00004B/1591